CLAYTON BYRD GOES
UNDERGROUND

CLAYTON BYRD
GOES UNDERGROUND

Rita Williams-Garcia
Illustrations by Frank Morrison

THORNDIKE PRESS
A part of Gale, a Cengage Company

A Cengage Company

Farmington Hills, Mich • San Francisco • New York • Waterville, Maine
Meriden, Conn • Mason, Ohio • Chicago

Recommended for Middle Readers.
Copyright © 2017 by Rita Williams-Garcia.
Illustrations copyright © 2017 by Frank Morrison.
Thorndike Press, a part of Gale, a Cengage Company.

ALL RIGHTS RESERVED
Thorndike Press® Large Print The Literacy Bridge.
The text of this Large Print edition is unabridged.
Other aspects of the book may vary from the original edition.
Set in 16 pt. Plantin.

LIBRARY OF CONGRESS CIP DATA ON FILE.
CATALOGUING IN PUBLICATION FOR THIS BOOK
IS AVAILABLE FROM THE LIBRARY OF CONGRESS

ISBN-13: 978-1-4328-5053-1 (hardcover)

Published in 2018 by arrangement with HarperCollins Children's Books,
a division of HarperCollins Publishers

Printed in Mexico
1 2 3 4 5 6 7 22 21 20 19 18

For Fred, who is the whole show

CONTENTS

WHEN, COOL PAPA, WHEN?

Clayton Byrd kept his eyes on Cool Papa Byrd. Cool Papa had a way with his electric blues guitar, Wah-Wah Nita. He could make her cry like no one else could.

While the crowd waited for one last song, Clayton waited for the sign. And then it came. First, dead silence. And then, instead of picking true notes on the strings, Cool Papa hit a few ghost notes, thumping his brass thumb ring against solid wood. He slid his thumb ring's edge along the metal strings. Electric blues sparks jumped out into the night.

The crowd in Washington Square Park ate it up. Hungry for the last bit of blues, the people clapped and called out, "Play that thang." Those ghostly thumps followed by twangy sparks teased the crowd. But for the Bluesmen and Clayton Byrd, the ghost notes laid out the song. Everything from chords, their order, and who would do what. The Bluesmen knew their parts. Clayton Byrd knew his.

Jack Rabbit Jones on keyboard laid down smooth chords with his left hand while the fingers on his right hand hip-hopped across the twelve-bar blues trail. Big Mike on bass walked the bottom bass line up and then down. Hector Santos kept the beat tight on percussion with two buckets, a brass hi-hat, and a snare drum. And Clayton Byrd on harmonica, a.k.a. the Mississippi saxophone, or what Cool Papa Byrd called the "blues harp," drew in and blew out as much life as he could between the musical spaces the Bluesmen left open for him.

When rhythm and slow-burning funk cooked into the blues, Cool Papa Byrd spoke-sang, deep and high, raspy and smooth:

"Trouble, don't you find me; Trouble, leave
    me alone.
I SAID, Trouble, keep your distance,
    Trouble, you better leave me alone.

Every time I think I kicked you to the curb,
   Trouble, I turn around and find you
   hanging on."

The wave of whoops from the crowd raised up into autumn air. It was like Cool Papa said. Happy people need the blues to cry, and sad people need the blues to laugh. And while the crowd clapped, called out, and boogied on that last song, Clayton found an opening to plead his case. His silver blues harp wedged in his mouth, his head cocked toward Cool Papa Byrd, Clayton Byrd drew more air in than out, asking,

"When, Cool Papa, when?
When, Cool Papa, when?
When, Cool Papa, when?"

When? — the last "when" blown into three pleading notes.

Instead of drowning out Clayton's plea with Wah-Wah Nita's full-bodied cry, Cool Papa answered back as only Cool Papa would. Cool. Clear. But sharp.

Not yet, Little Man, not yet.

Then louder. I SAID, Not yet, Little Man, not yet.

11

Softer — Not yet, Little Man, not yet.

Wait.

The Bluesmen smiled and played on. They'd heard this discussion between grandfather and grandson many times over. Even though Cool Papa and Wah-Wah Nita had answered, that didn't stop Clayton Byrd from hoping, and waiting.

All Clayton wanted was a twelve-bar solo — not even the twice-around-the-block solo that the other Bluesmen played. He wanted twelve bars and to be a true bluesman among bluesmen. Didn't Cool Papa tell the crowd earlier that the blues was more than a song, it was a story? Clayton knew that. Felt that. His lungs and soul were ready to pour out his own story through the ten square holes of his blues harp. He just needed Cool Papa Byrd to wave him in for a solo. Twelve bars. That was all.

Clayton counted twenty-four bars to each man's solo. He kept his arms at his sides, his ears open, his silver blues harp tight between his left thumb and pointer finger. His head bopped a light, steady groove. He could jump into the stream of blues like a fish since he was already in the musical swim of things.

So when Hector Santos, the last Blues-man, hit the brass hi-hat, twelve beats in a neat, tight buildup to finish his solo —

Clayton raised the silver harmonica to his lips, ready to draw in for that high pitch to start off his blues story.

But Cool Papa Byrd twanged in mightily and fiercely, told "Trouble" to "stay gone," and Clayton had no choice but to swallow the air for his solo and to come in with the Bluesmen on those final blues chords. Each voice faded out: keyboard, bass, percussion, blues harp, and blues guitar. The crowd went wild. Even better, every other person "dropped some greenback love," as Cool Papa would say, down into Wah-Wah Nita's open guitar case.

Clayton kept cool, although he felt himself getting a little hot inside. He had to keep cool if he was going to hang with Cool Papa and the Bluesmen. After all, his grandfather could have left him with his neighbor Omar's family. Or with his father, who wanted to field foul balls or show Clayton his baseball card collection. Clayton did those things with his father once a month. Once a month was enough.

Before it was completely dark, the Blues-men and Clayton boarded the uptown train with their instruments. They laughed among themselves and said the set was tight and the "take" was good.

Clayton agreed, but his cool had worn off. "Cool Papa. When do I get my solo?"

"Yeah, Cool Papa," Jack Rabbit Jones said. "He's in the union. Clayton, show 'im your union card." He meant his blues harp.

The Bluesmen laughed.

Clayton smiled but didn't laugh.

Cool Papa answered, "When you can bend that note proper, I'll wave you in. For now, just play rhythm. You'll be all right."

"I can bend it," Clayton said. He raised his harmonica to his lips, cupped his hand around his blues harp, and sucked in hard to show his grandfather. Riders on the train roused from their dead gazes. "You tell him, baby!" one lady shouted.

Big Mike cupped Clayton's head with fat, square fingers. "It's coming," he said. Jack Rabbit Jones and Hector Santos agreed.

Cool Papa disagreed. "No, son," he said with a smile in his eyes. "Not yet."

Big Mike said, "You gotta bend that note like you bend the truth."

Hector Santos said, "Like you bend backward, especially when you don't want to."

"Yeah, man," Jack Rabbit Jones said. "Gotta get that round-the-corner, back-to-tell-the-tale blues bend."

"Got to feel it deep down. In the gut," Cool Papa Byrd said. He patted himself somewhere between his heart and belly. "That's when you know you're crying."

"Just before you laugh," one said.

"Sometimes after," another said.

"But son," Cool Papa said, "a bluesman ain't a bluesman without that deep-down cry."

Clayton was full of questions and disappointments. His notes were good. True. He could reach high notes on one end of the harp, or run with the train in the middle notes, and draw in deep and way down for low notes. And he had a story. A blues story.

When Clayton couldn't stand it any longer, he said, "Why I have to bust a gut to be a bluesman? Why I gotta cry to get a solo?"

Clayton's outburst sent Cool Papa and the Bluesmen hollering. A few train riders chuckled.

"Don't think about it, Little Man," his grandfather said. "Don't think too hard. One day . . ."

"Or night," said Big Mike.

"It'll come," said Hector Santos.

"Just do what you're doing, Little Man," Cool Papa said. "Look sharp. Be cool. When it rains down on you, you won't have to ask because you'll be crying the blues on that harp."

"Amen," said the Bluesmen. "Amen to that."

Midnight Jam

The Bluesmen said Cool Papa and Clayton could find them either here or there, but they would most likely be in Washington Square Park for the next two or three weeks.

"After that we hit the road. You know how it is," said Hector Santos. "Warm weather."

Cool Papa gave each man a folded-greenback handshake from their take at the park. The Bluesmen said, "Later," at Forty-Second Street, then changed trains to hit a few blues clubs uptown. Cool Papa and Clayton stayed on the train that would take them home to Queens.

Clayton and Cool Papa tiptoed into the house just after nine and found the house quiet. Cool Papa gave a jolly and wicked

"Heh, heh, heh" laugh. "Looks like we made it."

"In the nick of time," Clayton agreed, and the two slapped hands.

Clayton washed up while Cool Papa threw a pot and a frying pan on the stove. In no time the house smelled like spaghetti and fish sticks, instead of the chewy and mushy three *p*'s Clayton's mother left for them: pork chops, peas, and potatoes.

Luckily, Ms. Byrd wasn't there to catch them sneaking in after a day of playing the blues in the park. Ms. Byrd had a low opinion of the blues. Almost as low an opinion as she had of her father, Clayton's grandfather. Whatever her reason, Clayton couldn't understand it. After all, the people in the park loved Cool Papa Byrd, and the Bluesmen looked to Cool Papa as a leader. So did Clayton. Cool Papa wasn't just Clayton's grandfather or a blues musician. He was Clayton's best friend, while Omar, who was Clayton's age, was his next best friend. Even with nearly six decades between the two Byrds, Clayton and Cool Papa had what Cool Papa called "harmony." He could tell Cool Papa anything and ask him anything. Around Cool Papa, Clayton didn't feel like a kid. He felt like a person.

Clayton looked forward to "double shift"

nights posted on the refrigerator door, held secure by one of his mother's many angel magnets. Whenever Ms. Byrd worked a double shift at the hospital on a Friday or Saturday night, Clayton and his grandfather snuck out to find the Bluesmen here or there, but mostly at Washington Square Park.

If Clayton's mother had any idea what the two had been up to, she'd let her father have it, but good — and probably kick him out of his own house. Clayton's ears picked up a lot when he was supposed to be asleep. He'd hear his mother scold her father and he'd hear his grandfather take it. She scolded Cool Papa for playing his blues records too loud and for wearing his shades inside the house. That made Clayton laugh to himself. He figured Cool Papa wore those shades indoors on purpose, just to hear her scolding voice. Cool Papa had a way about him that was fine with Clayton.

Clayton liked his father. Mr. Miller was all right. Nice, even. But Mr. Miller loved baseball. Science fiction. Jazz that sounded like angry elephants blowing their trumpets at each other. Mr. Miller tried to get Clayton to love those things too, but Clayton loved comic books. The blues. His blues harp. And Cool Papa Byrd.

"I want my solo," Clayton said. "I want the people to hear me play." He winked at his grandfather. "I know I'm good."

Cool Papa laughed. "Might be good, but you're not ready. You need seasoning."

"Aw, man!" Clayton balked, half joking, half whining. "Seasoning's for salt and pepper shakers."

"Precisely, man," his grandfather said back. "Blues gotta cook. Cooking and playing are the same thing."

Clayton fiddled with the angel-shaped shakers on the table, knocking one against the other.

"Look, son, I know the people in the park would drop more love in the guitar case if I waved you in. But I'm not raising you to be a cute kid."

Milk shot out of Clayton's nose. He wiped it with his pajama sleeve. Cute kid. He had to laugh.

"I'm raising you to be a bluesman," Cool Papa said. "Or just a man. But don't worry, man. I got my eye on you."

Clayton liked that. The way his grandfather broke it down, plain. Man to man. Even though he was a boy.

"I wasn't born cool like this," Cool Papa said in a way that could only be described as cool. "Before I was cool —"

Clayton heard this before and came in on cue: " 'I was hot. Mr. Louisiana Hot Lick.' "

"Got that right," Cool Papa said. "I had a road to travel and a life to live before I got this far. Mr. Louisiana Hot Lick had the good, raw stuff, like you. But you don't get any better than Cool Papa, and that takes time."

After they ate, Clayton brushed his teeth and got ready for the midnight jam, even though in reality, ten fifteen was closer to the hour. Clayton sat up in his bed, blues harp in hand, while Cool Papa Byrd pulled out First Guitar, a wide-bodied acoustic guitar that didn't need an amp and didn't glint like Show Guitar or cry like Wah-Wah Nita. First Guitar was on in years, and pluck-weary, but its strings produced the purest sound with a sweet echo on the end. She was perfect for the soft midnight jams.

Cool Papa sat at the foot of Clayton's bed in his "watcher's chair." That was what Clayton called his grandfather — his watcher. Someone who looked out for him.

Cool Papa tuned First Guitar and began picking an easy intro to lay out the chord changes. Clayton picked up the chord changes and joined in. Together, they played a sweet, sleepy blues riff. Sweet and low so neighbors wouldn't report them to Ms. Byrd, or to the police for disturbing the peace.

"One sheep over the meadow."

Clayton blew.

"Two sheep over the dale."

Clayton blew.

"Three sheep down by the river,
And four jump over the bed. . . ."

When the sweet notes faded to sleepy notes, Cool Papa nodded and said, "All right," which to Clayton was as good as applause. Cool Papa sat First Guitar on her stand, and Clayton shook the spit out of his blues harp, wiped it with his pajama sleeve, and tucked it under his pillow.

"Still wired up, son?"

"I guess," Clayton said, his eyes alert.

"All right. Strap in."

Cool Papa Byrd did what he'd always done after they jammed. He removed his dark shades, put on his reading glasses, and took the bedtime book from the shelf. There was nothing wrong with Clayton's reading.

He read just fine. He preferred Cool Papa's smooth, raspy voice, narrating the beckoning waves and the choppy waters. Both his mother and father said he was too old to be read to, but not Cool Papa. Besides, who better to read about embarking on travel and escaping trouble than Cool Papa, who had sailed the seas as a navy man, and traveled the road, both home and abroad, as a bluesman?

Clayton settled in.

No matter how much adventure the boy in the story, Pablo de Pablo, encountered, Clayton always fell asleep after the first few pages on double-shift nights. Within minutes that night, Clayton fell fast, dreaming of adventure.

Lost at Sea

The house settled under a quiet spell, broken only by the rubber marshmallow soles of Ms. Byrd's hospital shoes padding up the stairs, followed by the creaking of Clayton's bedroom door being pushed open.

Ms. Byrd peeked inside Clayton's room but didn't cross the threshold. Once again, her father and her son had fallen into a deep sleep. She felt a pinch of envy when she saw the book in her father's lap. He had never read to her.

"Angel," she said softly — and she didn't say this often about Clayton. As much as she refused to admit it, Mr. Miller, Clayton's father, was right: at times Clayton

Byrd could be a handful.

She wanted to kiss his cheek and forehead, but didn't. Instead, she stood at the door and watched her angel, his lids closed, the form of his body beneath the covers, rising and falling as he breathed in and out. She stood and watched her angel while he was that. Her angel.

The serene picture almost moved her to enter the room to kiss her father good night. But she hadn't kissed her father good night since she was a little girl. And even then, she didn't kiss him often, although she wanted to. Back then, Cool Papa Byrd had been light on the fathering side. He had been a brass-buttoned, polished navy officer. A navy officer on a ship, out to sea, sailing around the world. When his time with the navy was over, she hoped her father would drop anchor at their house and take her to baseball games. How she loved baseball stadiums! Or she hoped he would sit and have tea with her and her dollies. Or play his old guitar and sing happy songs to her and her mother. But instead, when her father's time with the navy was over, he went on the road with two of his flashy electric guitars. His old acoustic guitar was left behind, where it got kicked on angry birthdays. Cool Papa Byrd — which was what those blues-loving people called him — stayed on the road in blues clubs, honky-tonks, and juke joints, playing the blues with the Bluesmen. He would return home bearing gifts for Little Miss Byrd and her mother. He'd stay in their house for a month, maybe two. But as soon as a tour called his name, he'd pack up two of his three road guitars, his alligator boots, his fancy show vests, and his brown porkpie hat. He'd kiss his daughter and her mother and was once again gone for months and months. By the time Little Miss Byrd was Clayton's age, she hid from his kisses, wiped them away, and told anyone who asked that her father was lost at sea.

"No kisses for you, Papa," she whispered into the dark room. "No kisses tonight." And then she closed the door.

A SMALL WIND DANCE

The wind from the cracked window said, "Wake up, Clayton." Clayton turned over.

The wind blew around his ears, across his closed eyelids. "Wake up, Clayton. Wake up."

Finally, he did. Clayton stretched and opened his eyelids just as the violet of night turned pale blue and before white-yellow sun streams ran the pale blues out of the room.

Cool Papa still sat in his watcher's chair, the bedtime book in his lap.

There was something about how Clayton's grandfather looked to him, sitting in that chair. Something Clayton felt, but wasn't ready to know. Cool Papa's head and body were fully upright, his eyes on Clayton, but not with the same glint as when he sat in his watcher's chair and said, "Strap in, son," or "Clayton, I have my eye on you."

Clayton sat up. He took a breath, a deep one, then slipped out of his bed and stepped slowly toward Cool Papa. His heart thumped madly but he couldn't go any farther. Clayton stopped breathing. He inhaled sharply to force the breath out of him until he was breathing more in — quick and jagged — than out. He could taste the sour sickness in his stomach. When his breathing was almost normal, Clayton took another step and waited. His was the only breathing he heard.

When he took the last step, he bent down to be eye to eye with his grandfather. But he bent down mainly because his legs were weak.

"Cool Papa . . ." he whispered.

The bedtime book rested in Cool Papa's lap, his shades in his breast pocket. His reading glasses had fallen to the carpet.

Clayton looked into Cool Papa Byrd's eyes, to see if Cool Papa still had his eyes on him. He looked into the liquid brown, and saw himself. He stood a moment longer.

Clayton put his hand on Cool Papa's face. At first, just the fingertips, and then his whole hand. Cool Papa Byrd's face was hard and tough, not soft and tough, like Clayton had known it to be.

He stroked his hand along Cool Papa's jaw. His grandfather's skin was cold.

The curtain blew a small wind dance through the cracked window. Clayton Byrd didn't have to be told. Instead, he'd be the one to tell his mother Cool Papa Byrd was gone.

THE SKY IS CRYING

Ms. Byrd and Clayton sat in the very front pew of the church, across from Cool Papa Byrd's long, polished oak coffin.

Ms. Byrd didn't cry, so Clayton didn't cry, even though sadness filled almost every inch of his being. No matter how badly he felt, he couldn't start crying. He didn't want anyone to see him cry and feel sorry for him. Most important, he had a plan, and he couldn't carry it out if his nose was full of snot and his throat was choked up. Clayton had slipped his blues harp in his pocket while he was getting dressed. Instead of reading a poem or a farewell letter like Omar had read at his grandfather's funeral, Clayton decided to say his farewell in a simple blues scale in G. Blues in G was the first scale he learned and accompanied Cool Papa on. It was the scale of the sleepy midnight jams. Clayton had practiced for a week. He knew what he'd say in his twenty-four bars and how he'd say it.

He didn't tell his mother about his planned farewell. He knew she wouldn't approve. Even worse, he knew his mother would forbid blues-playing of any kind. He kept his blues harp in his jacket pocket and rubbed his fingers across the holes every now and again.

Clayton and his mother sat in the pews meant for family on the right-hand side of the church. Behind them sat Clayton's grand-aunts and -uncles, many second cousins, and a slew of relatives. On the left-hand side in the front row sat the Bluesmen, all looking sharper than seven sharps in the key of C.

When Clayton had met the Bluesmen a few years ago, he thought their middle names were "On." Cool Papa Byrd had said, "This is Jack Rabbit Jones on keyboard, Big Mike on bass, and Hector Santos on percussion." His grandfather, of course, was Cool Papa Byrd on blues guitar. The Bluesmen agreed that they could sure use a man on blues harp. From then on, Cool Papa Byrd taught Clayton to blow the harmonica out to make it shout, and to draw in his breath to make it shudder or chug like a train.

Behind the Bluesmen sat three lovely ladies in hats. All carried hankies in their fat dimpled hands. They out-cried Ms. Byrd and Clayton, and all of Cool Papa Byrd's family seated on the right-hand side of the church.

Behind the three lovely ladies sat Cool Papa Byrd's shipmates from the navy, their gold buttons gleaming against their dark-blue jackets. Or as Cool Papa Byrd would have said, "Man, they were shipshape."

Behind the navy men sat a few of Cool Papa Byrd's classmates from his school days. And even his old math teacher.

Behind the mourners from school days' past sat the throng of people who had heard and loved his electric blues guitar licks. And then behind them sat a few people who, by the looks of them, hoped sandwiches would be served later.

Last, Mr. Miller, Clayton's father, entered the church. He strode down the aisle and filed into the front pew where the family sat. He kissed Clayton's mother on her cheek. A quick hello kiss. Hello with sorrow. He patted Clayton on the back and sat next to him.

"You all right, son?" his father asked.

"I'm cool," Clayton answered.

"Clayton!" Ms. Byrd scolded. "Don't forget where you are." She shook her head, short and curt. "You sound like your grandfather."

And that made Clayton smile in his heart.

Then the organist began to fill the church with organ sounds. It wasn't the music of the blues clubs. The honky-tonks. Their secret Washington Square Park concerts. Or their midnight jams. It was the music Ms. Byrd instructed the organist to play. "A heavenly tune," she'd told the organist, although Ms. Byrd didn't believe her father would go straight to heaven. He had made too many people cry — especially her mother — to go straight to heaven. Her father's soul had a long road to travel.

The Bluesmen had come ready to play. A send-off wouldn't be a party without the blues to ferry Cool Papa Byrd on his journey.

They offered to play a tribute, but Ms. Byrd thanked them kindly and firmly and said, "No blues music of any kind."

The Bluesmen were not pleased, but kept their cool.

So the organist played hymns. The preacher preached. The lovely ladies boohooed. And Clayton fiddled with the folded paper that told the story of Cool Papa Byrd's life, read by one of Cool Papa Byrd's brothers.

Clayton hoped to hear funny stories about his grandfather as a kid, or as a young musician during his "Mr. Louisiana Hot Lick" days, or of his days at sea in the navy. He hoped to hear about the Cool Papa he knew, and how he got to be so cool.

Instead, Uncle Clifton Byrd read the date that Clayton's grandfather had been born. He read that he had brothers and sisters — who began to cry. That he had married and was joining his wife in heaven. (Ms. Byrd uttered a "hmp" that Clayton, his father, and the preacher heard.) Uncle Clifton read that he and his wife had one daughter, Clayton's mother, and one grandson, Clayton Byrd. Then Clayton's father muttered, "Clayton Miller." Ms. Byrd's fingers rose to her lips.

Cool Papa's brother read a list of schools he had attended. Named the church he belonged to and said that he was an officer in the navy. To that, Cool Papa's navy mates lifted their hats and shouted, "Hoorah!"

But the folded paper with a beautiful sunset did not mention one word about the blues. The big concerts he opened and closed, the songs he wrote, and the famous musicians he toured with. There was nothing about his oldest friend — First Guitar; or his glitzy Show Guitar that had been custom-made for his style of playing; or his funky, hard-crying guitar, Wah-Wah Nita, the guitar he played the most. There was also no mention of his time on the road with the Bluesmen. There was no mention of his grandson, Clayton Byrd, as his blues protégé. That was because the name on the folded paper was not Cool Papa Byrd, as he was known on the blues circuit, uptown and downtown. The name printed on the folded paper with the setting sun and praying hands was Herman Clayton Byrd.

The Bluesmen, the lovely ladies in hats, the people who loved his blues guitar-playing had all read the folded paper and were not pleased. Murmurs of "Do you see this?" and "How could she?" rustled through the pews.

Ms. Byrd made no particular facial expression to the murmurs and rustling from the left-hand side of the church.

At last, when the eulogist finished eulogizing, the preacher finished preaching, and the organist finished playing heavenly hymns, the preacher asked if anyone would like to say a few words. Jack Rabbit Jones on keyboard stood up. Big Mike on bass stood up. And Hector Santos on percussion stood. So, naturally, Clayton Byrd on blues harp also stood. But he was quickly and firmly pulled down to his seat. Small stabs of anger pricked at him. She had killed his plan.

Then the Bluesmen gathered around the speaker's mic and sang a blues song, "The Sky Is Crying." When they finished singing, Jack Rabbit Jones took off his shades, walked over to the long, polished oak coffin where Cool Papa Byrd's body rested, and placed the shades over Cool Papa Byrd's closed eyes.

Only then did Clayton smile on the outside.

Takers

Clayton kept the window cracked open just in case Cool Papa decided to breeze on through. He knew his grandfather's body had been buried in the cemetery. He'd seen the oak casket lowered into the ground with Cool Papa's body inside. But he wasn't certain about his grandfather's spirit and where it went. Clayton's list of what he believed in was short, but he held out a small hope that Cool Papa, like music, was in the air, and Clayton didn't want to miss his last chance to feel him near.

The next morning Clayton awoke in a foul mood and found it hard to stay wrapped in his blanket, with sunbeams streaming into his room. It might as well have been a school day instead of Saturday. He planned to stay indoors, and under his blanket. He'd tell his mother he was sick, but there was noise rising up into his room, noise that had nothing to do with his grandfather's roaming spirit.

Clayton poked his head out from his blanket to hear what was stirring below. He got out of bed and pressed his forehead against the window. There were people in his yard. Neighbors and strangers milling. Looking. Carrying things away. Cool Papa's things.

A charge shot through Clayton, from the blood beneath his skin to the tips of his toenails. He got out of his pajamas and into his jeans, pullover, and sneakers and was dashing down the stairs and out into the yard to stop the takers.

A man rifled through his grandfather's crate of record albums. Cool Papa had promised the collection to Clayton, even though Clayton didn't have the right player for the large black discs. Still, they were his, and he was on a mission to stop the man from taking them.

The man must have seen Clayton spring out of the house, because he asked him right away, "Son, how much for the records? Right fine treasures." The man wasn't from around the neighborhood. He had a cowboy twang that Clayton would have liked if he hadn't been one of the takers.

"They're not for sale," Clayton told the man.

His mother, who'd been showing ladies souvenirs from places Cool Papa had traveled, stopped talking and turned her head toward Clayton and the man. She left the ladies with the knickknacks and sped over. "They're all for sale, mister," she said. "Every last one."

"You can't!" Clayton said.

"Bob," the man told Ms. Byrd.

Ms. Byrd said, "They're all for sale, Bob. Take the whole crate." She looked to the sky. "Ten dollars."

"You can't!" Clayton said louder, although that didn't matter.

Bob looked at Ms. Byrd with big, astonished eyes. "Madam," he said politely, flipping through the flat cardboard covers, "why, there's Bessie. Billie. Rosetta. Son. Robert. B.B. King, Albert King, and Alberta King. And Howlin' Wolf, too! And there's Stevie Ray! Madam, are you sure you know what you're giving away?"

"I know what they are," Clayton's mother sang flatly — but not in the flat notes that gave the blues its funk.

"Tell you what." Bob's voice was cowboy

39

twangy and amazed. "I'll give you fifty. Only way I can sleep at night — and I might still toss and turn."

"Suit yourself," Clayton's mother said.

"That's not right," Clayton told his mother. "Those are Cool Papa's blues people. He meant them for me!"

"It's old stuff, Clayton. And it's taking up too much space. It's gotta go."

It didn't matter. People continued to fill Clayton's front yard. They saw the sign *Yard Sale — All Must Go!* and stopped their jogging, bike riding, and dog walking. Ms. Byrd gave them whatever they offered for Cool Papa's treasures. Sometimes she said, "Just take it."

"Great stuff!" Omar exclaimed. At that moment, "friend" was the last thing Clayton would have called Omar. Omar pinned one of Cool Papa's navy medals to his T-shirt and plopped Cool Papa's navy cap on his head. The front slunk down over Omar's eyes, which Omar thought was funny.

Clayton could have bashed his face in.

"Take that off," Clayton said.

"Nope."

"Take it off."

"I paid a quarter. It's mine."

Clayton didn't bash Omar's face in like he wanted to, but shoved him instead. Hard.

Omar stumbled backward.

"What's the big idea?" Omar shouted.

Clayton was too angry to answer. And he was on a mission. He had to stop the takers from walking away with his grandpa's treasures.

They'd ask how much and Clayton would say, "Not for sale." Then his mother would scold him and sell Cool Papa's treasures anyway.

No matter what he did or said, he couldn't stop the takers. There were too many, and his mother kept accepting their few dollars or few coins.

A shaggy-haired teen walked away with Cool Papa's showtime alligator boots — the ones he always wore onstage with Show Guitar. A woman older than Clayton's mother tried on Cool Papa's showtime vest, "oohed" in F major, and hollered, "I must have it!" But when a young woman picked up Cool Papa's porkpie hat and placed it on her head, Clayton couldn't stop himself. He set eyes on his target, crouched low, and with a running start, jumped high, because she was tall, and snatched the porkpie hat off her head. "Not for sale!" he snapped at her. He might have hurt the young woman. He might have tugged on her hair, because she cried "Ouch!" and walked away.

41

His hands were awfully angry.

Ms. Byrd had seen enough, and came toward him. Like Clayton's angry hands, his mother's feet and face were awfully angry.

Clayton ran into the house, up the stairs, and inside his room and slammed the door.

"Stay in there!" his mother called up to him. "Stay until I say you can come out."

Clayton hurled the porkpie hat high up on a shelf in his closet. He fell on his bed and mumbled, "I don't care," among other things.

It was a bad Saturday morning, on the verge of getting worse. But Clayton didn't know the worst of it until it happened.

He got out of his bed to see if the takers had gone. He pressed his forehead against the window pane and looked down. One by one he saw the takers: The first walked out of his yard with Cool Papa's First Guitar. The second had Cool Papa's Show Guitar. And the last taker had Wah-Wah Nita slung over his back as he carried her out of the gate. Clayton could hear her crying, *wah-wah*. But he didn't cry with her. He just let his crying boil up inside him.

Empty Room

The people had all left once the sun began to set. By then everything was gone and the Yard Sale signs had been taken down from the garage door and front lawn.

Clayton's mother called up, "Clayton. Dinner!"

Clayton's stomach growled. He had eaten only half a box of old Red Hots that had lost their zing, and a pack of stale and crumbly peanut butter crackers nearly forgotten in his book bag. Peanut butter crackers were bad for playing the blues harp, but they were okay after a day of anger and starvation.

He emerged from his room, then stood in

the hallway, just outside Cool Papa Byrd's room. The narrow, empty room once belonged to Cool Papa and Grandma Irene, but she died first and all of her things had been taken away. The disappearance of his grandmother's dresses, hats, sewing machine, and gardening books didn't bother Clayton. In fact, he'd helped his mother put her things in boxes for the church rummage sale. She had been so sick, he was relieved when his mother told him his grandmother was gone. It was different with Cool Papa's things. Why his mother didn't understand that, Clayton didn't know.

Clayton entered.

The room, stripped of almost every trace of his grandparents, made its own hollow quiet. Clayton whispered, "Why, Cool Papa, why?" His voice, wrapped in the quiet, bounced off the walls, echoing the emptiness of the room. All that was left was Cool Papa's hat rack, the bare bed, and an oak dresser. The dresser was the resting place for the framed photograph of Cool Papa Byrd, Grandma Irene, and First Guitar. It was strange to see Cool Papa and Grandma Irene so young. Young, before they had Clayton's mother, and long before they had become grandparents. Clayton never liked the mushy song about the wings of love, but

44

he could see his grandparents once had the kind of happiness that had wings. Young Cool Papa and Grandma Irene looked happy, like they could fly away.

It was strange to see the hat rack in the corner with no hat. Cool Papa Byrd had owned many a hat, but mainly wore the brown felt brim porkpie hat.

A wave of satisfaction swept through Clayton now that he had the hat safely out of reach in his closet. If he felt sorry for snatching the porkpie hat from the tall lady earlier that morning, the few pangs of regret were now gone. Instead, now he was mad. And hungry.

When he came to the table where his dinner plate cooled, his mother asked, "Did you wash your hands?"

"Yeah," he said. But he was lying.

"Say grace, Clayton." His mother didn't clasp her hands, but she bowed her head.

Clayton lowered his head, but only because he didn't want to face his mother eye to eye. And he felt down. Low and down. "Grace," he grumbled, and picked up his meat by the bone and took a big chomp, then chewed, mostly with his mouth open. Knowing how his mother felt about table manners, Clayton wiped his mouth with his sleeve rather than using the embroidered cloth napkin still folded at the left-hand side of his plate.

"Keep it up and you'll be sorry," his mother said.

Clayton took an even bigger chomp than before. He hadn't eaten all day and was truly hungry. And angry. "I don't care."

His mother calmly picked up her knife and fork and cut firm strips of meat from the bone. "Keep it up," she said, "and there'll be no more gaming. No science museum with your father. And no harmonica. Keep it up."

"It's a blues harp."

His mother exhaled, put her fork down, and stared at her son in utter disbelief. She picked up the angel saltshaker as if it were precious and tapped it lightly over her food. Clayton had once dropped the shaker, breaking the tip of one of its wings. His mother had glued it back on.

"I know you miss your grandfather, but that's no excuse for acting like some little demon."

Clayton laughed at that. *Little demon.* What would she call him if he threw the glass salt and pepper angels across the room? What could she do that was worse than getting rid of all of Cool Papa's things?

"I don't think what you did was right,"

Clayton told his mother. "You gave away everything without asking me."

"I told you," she said. "There's no room for that old stuff."

"You let them take the guitars."

"He can't play them anymore, Clayton," she said plainly. "It's better to sell them to people who can't afford to buy them brand-new."

"I can play them," he lied. He couldn't play the guitar. But he planned to learn, even though his school didn't offer music lessons for kids who wanted to play instruments. Clayton planned to learn how to play the guitar and how to tune the strings, hold the neck and body the way Cool Papa did, and eventually read music charts and play the notes. "You don't even know what Cool Papa called his guitars."

"It doesn't matter what he called them. They're gone to new owners who can call them whatever name they like. And if you care so much about his name, why don't you honor your grandfather by calling him something respectful, like Grandpa Herman. After all, you are his only grandchild."

How did she do that? Clayton wondered. How did she make herself right and him wrong? He didn't have an answer for himself and he didn't have an answer to give her. A cool answer that would have made her stop talking and feel bad. As bad as he felt. Clayton did the next best thing to giving an answer, and chewed until meat fell out of his mouth. He picked it up with his hands and ate it.

THE FOUR CORNERS
OF THE WORLD

That Monday morning, part of Clayton felt
blue and wanted to stay at home, under his
blanket. The other part of Clayton was
ready to return to school after having been
away for seven whole days. Clayton stashed
his silver harp beneath his pillow. He ate his
breakfast, grabbed his book bag, and said
"Bye" to his mother.

"Remember," his mother called after him,
"go straight to Omar's after school."

Clayton didn't turn around.

He and Omar slugged each other hello
and boarded the school bus. Clayton decided he was no longer angry at his friend,
and that seemed to be good enough for
Omar.

When he entered his classroom, his teacher, Ms. Treadwell, said, "Welcome back, Clayton." Her eyes were kind and bright, but not sorry. He had had enough of people giving him sorry eyes, or even worse, telling him they were sorry about his grandfather.

He took his seat in the last row, glad to find everything where he'd left it. Luckily, his desk was next to the table where the lizard's cage sat. The lizard, who was never named, didn't venture out often from his rock den among the Egyptian clover, but when he did, it took every ounce of Clayton's strength to not watch the lizard dart between the clover.

The class began the day as they always had, with glee. Starting the day by singing from *The Great American Book of Glee* was one of Clayton's favorite parts of the day. Since their school didn't offer band or lessons on musical instruments, Ms. Treadwell let Clayton accompany the class on his blues harp a few times — something he'd never told his mother. This morning, however, Clayton neither sang nor played along when the class sang "You Are My Sunshine." They sang so joyfully loud that Ms. Katz from across the hall tapped on their door's window and motioned for less volume. Ms. Treadwell smiled her apology to Ms. Katz and the class sang on, but softer. Without Clayton.

Clayton knew the words. He even liked the song. He simply refused to sing a song done wrong. The gleeful rendition had never bothered him before, but this morning it upset his ears. "Sunshine" wasn't a fast, loud, and gleeful song. No matter how fast it was sung, "Sunshine" wanted to be happy but underneath felt blue.

After recess, the class usually laid their heads on their desks while Ms. Treadwell read aloud in her storytelling voice. Instead, Ms. Treadwell announced, "Today we begin our new journey."

The class celebrated with yays and yesses, but Clayton pounded his fist on his desk. Ms. Treadwell had finished reading "The Rime of the Ancient Mariner" while he had been on leave.

Ms. Treadwell pulled down the map of the world that had been rolled above the board. It wasn't the flat drawings of the seven continents and five oceans that caught Clayton's eye, but the construction-paper model of a boat and a boy, taped to the middle of the ocean that Clayton saw first. He knew the small boat and its lone crew member. He knew their story.

"Hey!"

Ms. Treadwell held up the book that showed the same figures: a boy at sea on a small boat. Murmurs of excitement swept around the room. Normally, Ms. Treadwell would have told the class to quiet down, but not today.

Without raising his hand, Clayton said, "I read that book already."

Ms. Treadwell replied, "There's nothing wrong with reading it again."

"Can I read something else?"

"No, Clayton. We'll all read together and do group projects. Now, remember to raise your hand for permission to speak." The twinkle in her eye encouraged him to want to do better.

Clayton raised his hand, but didn't wait to be called on. "But I don't want to read it again."

Ms. Treadwell's eyes stopped smiling.

"Clayton, you know how this works. Raise your hand, and wait to be called on."

His classmates' snickering trickled around him. Clayton put his head on his desk, his outburst ignored. Instead, Ms. Treadwell talked about the book, the project, and the boy and boat. She wrote words on the board: *gaggle of geese, bee swarm, whale pod, wolf pack,* and *murder of crows.* Everyone except Clayton seemed enthused about the journey.

Baskets of the blue paperback books traveled from front row to back row until everyone had a copy of *The Four Corners of the World* on their desk. Ms. Treadwell said, "Open your books and your notebooks. If you come to a word you don't know, write it in your notebook. When you finish chapter one, put your book in the basket and your head down on your desk. Everyone ready?" she asked the class, but she didn't expect a real answer. All eyes were eager, except for Clayton's.

"Read!" she said, as if signaling the start of a relay.

This was no relay.

Why Clayton couldn't choose his own book, he didn't understand. He wasn't fond of group projects. Last year for the earthworm project, he'd been stuck with some kids who didn't want to touch worms and another kid who kept trying to force everyone to eat the worms. Group projects were dumb. They weren't like jamming with the Bluesmen, knowing when to come in, how to play against and with other musicians. Now that was a group!

Clayton looked over at the lizard's cage

and searched for the small reptile, but couldn't find him. Then he saw movement beneath the plant leaves. A quick movement followed by stillness. The lizard's skin coloring had blended into the white, violet, and green of the Egyptian clover. Now he could see the lizard's head, and only one black bead of an eye, which meant the lizard could see him. He thought it was cool and creepy the way a lizard's eyes could see on both sides of its head.

"Eh-um."

Ms. Treadwell's throat-clearing was directed his way. Clayton got the message and opened the book on his desk.

Pablo de Pablo's lot in life was simple and predestined.

Most of Clayton's classmates were neatly writing "predestined" in their notebooks. Clayton didn't touch his pen. He knew what it meant, and once more, he had the sound of his grandfather's voice creating meaning in his ear. Predestined.

His life would be the same as his father's, his father's father's, and without a doubt, his father's father's father's.

Clayton chuckled. He had no dreams to

follow his own father's destiny. Who'd want to be a loan officer in a bank?

But none of the fates written in the stars were of any concern to Pablo de Pablo. He heard the call of the sea once he laid eyes on its gleaming crests. Unlike his father, his father's father, and his father's father's father, Pablo de Pablo was destined to journey to the four corners of the world.

Clayton continued on, the words familiar and soothing, rolling melodically around inside his mind as he read. And before he knew it, his eyes grew heavy and his neck wobbly. He turned the page, and then put his head down on the cool surface of his desk. Before long, Clayton was sound asleep.

He didn't know that his neighbor Alma was pointing at him or that he was snoring. Clayton had fallen into a hard sleep. So hard he didn't hear the *clack-clump* of Ms. Treadwell's shoes hitting the floor, heading his way.

"Clayton," she said both softly and sternly.

The classroom filled with laughter. That was what woke Clayton up — the laughter of his classmates.

Blues Day

The next day Clayton awoke determined to work on his goodness. He wanted to fall into the groove of things, so he sang "This Land Is Your Land" along with his class for glee. He raised his hand and waited to be called on before speaking. He didn't whine when it was time for silent reading, even though he knew practically every word in chapter two, "The Call to Adventure," by heart. He could hear his grandfather's voice, reading:

"The call of the sea pulled him closer to its tempting edge. Adventure! Adventure, the waves called. Let us show you the world, Pablo de Pablo. Explore!"

Clayton opened his eyes wide. He leaned forward as if to lean into the story as the boy set off on his journey to one of the far corners of the world. He was doing well and read silently, rapidly, picturing the boy in the boat mastering the tide.

Soon the motion of the green-blue sea, its flickering crests, sent him sailing toward drowsiness. He fought the urge to give in, but his eyes glazed. The words on the page blurred. Before Pablo de Pablo, boy explorer, could establish command of his little boat, Clayton's head sank down upon his desk, and he fell into the deepest sleep.

Alma tapped his leg with her sneaker, but Clayton only turned his head to the other side. A small wad of paper hit his ear. He scratched his ear and continued to snore, now, louder. Ms. Treadwell's chair scraped against the floor, but she didn't awaken Clayton. Nor did the sound of her heels. Clayton snored even louder, which made the class laugh louder. His teacher bent slightly, and placed her hand on his shoulder. She spoke softly.

"Clayton Byrd."

One eyelid rolled up. Clayton looked around slowly. He was no longer in a boat out to sea, but in a row of desks and chairs. He tossed aside his oar, yawned until his ravioli-and-string-bean breath hit Ms. Treadwell. She blinked.

"Clayton. See me after class."

The room echoed with "Oohs". Clayton shrugged. He didn't mean to fall asleep. He knew why. He just couldn't say why *The Four Corners of the World* put him to sleep. Or that his grandfather died with *The Four Corners of the World* in his lap. Clayton couldn't. Wouldn't. Open. His. Mouth.

"About time," his bus driver said when he finally climbed aboard.

Clayton said, "Sorry," and then slid into the seat Omar had saved for him.

"Alma told me what happened," Omar said.

Clayton stood and looked for Alma. She caught his eye and stuck out her tongue. Like the lizard. He sat back down.

"What did Ms. Treadwell say?" Omar asked.

"Nothing much," Clayton said, although that was far from true. Ms. Treadwell asked him if he was getting enough sleep at home, to which he answered yes. She asked if there was a particular reason why he was tired. He shook his head and answered no. And that was true. He wasn't tired for any particular reason. Then she told him in her special and gentle voice that she understood he was going through a rough time, but he'd have to stay awake in class. Especially during reading. He asked again if he could read a different book — any other book than the one she assigned. Ms. Treadwell smiled and said, "Nice try, Clayton, but no. No, you may not." She said, "Tomorrow is a new day," and that she wanted to see improvement.

"Oh," Omar said, disappointed. "That's all?"

Clayton took an envelope out of his book bag.

"You got a note?"

Clayton raised his eyebrows and shrugged.

"You going to show it to your mother?"

Another shrug.

Clayton had played it off cool with Omar and the few classmates who laughed at him on the bus ride home. It had been the second day in a row that Clayton had fallen asleep during reading, and his classmates soon forgot that he was the kid whose grandfather died, or even the kid who played the harmonica. Clayton's snoring became legendary. His new name was "Sleepster."

Their teasing didn't seem to bother him.

Clayton grabbed his book bag as soon as his mother pulled into their driveway.

"Be strong," Omar said, half teasing.

Clayton shrugged. "Later." He said "Bye" to Omar's mom and was out the back door, striding toward his mother. She looked tired.

"Hey, Mom."

"Hey, angel."

He didn't waste time. She was tired, but she had called him "angel." As soon as they entered their house, and she sighed heavily, Clayton pulled out the folded letter from his book bag.

"What's this?" she asked. Clayton noted she wasn't angry yet.

He raised his eyebrows and shrugged.

"Clayton . . ." She whipped the paper open. He watched her eyes race across and down the paper. It took her all of three two-count musical bars to read the letter.

He braced himself for scolding.

"Why are you sleeping in class, angel?"

Clayton's eyebrows raised. He shrugged. "I don't know. I want to read a different book. That's all."

"Clayton, you don't get to do what you

want. You do what your teacher says. You know better."

He didn't shrug. But he didn't speak, either.

She exhaled, and then seemed to wait a full two four-count bars before saying, "Tomorrow you're staying home."

Clayton wished he had read the letter. "Why am I staying home? Am I suspended?"

His mother, who usually answered without fixing her words first, hesitated before speaking. Finally she said, "You have to speak to someone before you return to class."

What does that mean? he thought.

"Did you have your snack?" she asked.

He nodded yes.

"Finish your homework?"

"Not all of it."

"Get it done," she said. "And Clayton . . ."

"Yeah?"

"I don't want to hear any harmonica playing tonight or I'll take that thing away."

He didn't remind her it was a blues harp.

HOUSE OF GOD

Clayton listened as carefully as he could while his parents spoke on the phone. It was hard to understand everything when he could only hear his mother's voice, and not even every word she said. From what he gathered, both Ms. Byrd and Mr. Miller agreed that he had to talk to someone before he returned to school, but that was as far as their agreement went. His mother said, "A grief counselor?" as if his father suggested he speak to a witch doctor. And after his mother said Pastor Early's name, he heard nothing, which meant his father was speaking. Then his mother's voice became firmer than firm, and that was followed by more silence. And then there was no talking at all.

This no-talking-at-all business didn't surprise Clayton. His parents seldom spoke to each other for long, even though Mr. Miller had moved from his city apartment to be closer to the Byrds' home. Clayton couldn't imagine his parents holding hands. They were nothing like the happy young couple in the frame that sat on Cool Papa's oak dresser. Ms. Byrd and Mr. Miller seemed completely alien to each other. How he had come into being, Clayton couldn't figure.

As with most things, Ms. Byrd got her way. Instead of hopping on the school bus with Omar, the next day Clayton found himself waiting to speak to Pastor Early.

Clayton thought only he was being made to talk to someone, although he didn't want to talk to Pastor Early or anyone else. But there he sat on the bench outside Pastor Early's study while his mother spoke to the pastor first, and for too long a time.

Clayton grew tired of sitting and waiting. He pulled out his blues harp. There was a hymn they sang in church that he liked. What Cool Papa called a "southern hymn." He played softly, but drew in deeply to sink the notes low and hard, just short of bending them to make the song truly bluesy. It might as well have been a blues song, the way it asked a question that needed an answer.

What wondrous love is this, oh my soul?

Clayton closed his eyes and spun the melody farther and farther away from its simple original tune. He wondered about the moment that Cool Papa left his body behind. As he got further into his blues-soaked answer, the door opened and his mother stepped out of Pastor Early's office. Her face was red and swollen.

Clayton wanted to say something nice or comforting to her, but she wiped her eyes quickly.

"Clayton! Where do you think you are, playing that music?" If her voice was at all shaky, it was now steady.

Pastor Early said in his booming pulpit voice, "Who's making that fine, fine music out there?" He stood at the door.

"Give me that thing," his mother said.

Clayton shoved his blues harp in his pocket.

"Had one just like it," Pastor Early said, trying to coax a smile out of Clayton. "Come on in, son. Have a seat." Then to Ms. Byrd, he said, "We'll be a few minutes," and he closed the door.

"I understand your grandfather was a fine musician."

"Bluesman," Clayton said.

"Indeed," the pastor said. "Indeed."

When Clayton was younger, about six, he thought Pastor Early was God. His mother said one Sunday that they were going to the house of God, and Clayton was anxious to see him. After all, Clayton was made to pray to Him before he ate and before he slept. It was about time he'd actually see this God. Sure enough, when they arrived, the big man with the big voice said "Welcome to the house of God" to Clayton, his mother, and all the visitors. It was after the service, when he asked Pastor Early to marry his father and mother, that he had learned the truth. He stood before the pastor and shouted, "You said there was nothing God wouldn't give! 'Ask and it shall be given.' " His mother scolded him, but Pastor Early laughed heartily and said, "I'm glad you were listening, son, but —"

Clayton didn't want to hear the "but." He cut off the pastor and asked, "Aren't you all-powerful and all-knowing?" His mother was embarrassed and cried out, "Clayton!"

From then on, Clayton attended church every Sunday because he was being made to go. He joined the children's choir to be close to music that sounded like the blues his grandfather played. But Clayton didn't listen to the sermons, and he said "amen" only when it was a word in a song.

Clayton sat down but had nothing to say.

"How are you feeling, young man?"

"Okay," Clayton said.

"You don't have to say you're okay if you're not," the pastor said.

Clayton said nothing. He looked around the office. There was one nice thing on the pastor's desk. A perfect cube made up of smaller cubes. Blue, yellow, orange, green, red, and white. A Rubik's Cube. He'd heard of them, and now he was staring at one.

Clayton, who was typically cool, was thoroughly drawn to the object.

Pastor Early nodded. "Go ahead. Hold it. Figure it out."

Clayton didn't hesitate. He took it, tossed it up for a quick catch to see if it came apart, and then he began twisting and turning the colored cubes. He started with blue, his favorite color.

While he worked on the cube, Pastor Early explained why Cool Papa died and what happened next. He spoke mainly about suffering and being released from suffering. Being called home "when it's your time."

The pastor was wrong, Clayton thought. Cool Papa Byrd didn't beg to be released from earthly suffering. He hadn't been sick or wasting away like Grandma Irene. He didn't take pills. Didn't need an oxygen tank, a cane, a walker. Didn't have emergencies. He might have been older than most people Clayton knew, but Cool Papa wasn't old or weak. He could get down with his electric guitar in Washington Square Park and make the crowd holler for more. One night he was reading the bedtime book from the watcher's chair with his eye on Clayton. By early morning he was gone. But he was never sick or suffering, nor did he pray to be released or to be called home.

Not like Grandma Irene. She had gotten so sick that Cool Papa had come off the road for good to stay with her. Every day Clayton asked his mother, "Did she die yet?" Clayton's mother only said, "No, angel," until one day she just cried and cried.

After Grandma Irene's funeral, Clayton had returned to first grade like nothing had happened. In fact, he was happy. Happy they kept the lid closed on her coffin, because she had long ago stopped looking like herself. He couldn't tell his mother those things, but he told Cool Papa. And Cool Papa said, "Little Man, I know just what you mean." And then Cool Papa taught him his first blues scale on the harp.

But that wasn't how Cool Papa had left him. And there was no one to tell about how he felt about Cool Papa leaving. Even if Pastor Early repeated what Cool Papa had said — *"Little Man, I know just what you mean"* — Clayton doubted the pastor knew anything.

No, Clayton told himself. It wasn't Cool Papa's time. It wasn't.

But somewhere in all of his talking, the pastor said the word *road,* as in "making our own journey on the road of life," and something clicked! Something he'd been told at Cool Papa's farewell. It was a miracle! The pastor said the magic word, and the final cube twisted into place.

"Right!" Clayton told himself. Or so he thought.

The pastor only smiled and continued talking.

By the winding-down tones in Pastor Early's voice, Clayton knew his time sitting across from the pastor was coming to an end. It was like counting and hearing the chord changes. He could always hear the changes in the music, know what it meant and what he had to do.

He put the cube down.

When he stepped outside the pastor's office, his mother was right there. She'd forgotten about taking Clayton's blues harp away and kissed him on the forehead, which he wiped with his jacket sleeve.

"You feel better, angel?"

Clayton shrugged.

She thanked the pastor for giving them his time and said, "What do you say, Clayton?"

Clayton turned around, stuck out his hand, and when Pastor Early shook it, Clayton said, "Good-bye."

"Clayton! Say thank you! Say, 'Thank you, Pastor Early.' "

He didn't understand why he was thanking the pastor, but he understood his mother was mad and embarrassed and would blame his blues harp for his rudeness.

"Thanks, man," Clayton said.

"You're welcome, man," the pastor said back. To both Clayton and Ms. Byrd he said, "Next time, I want to see you both. Together."

Ms. Byrd made the same silence as Clayton. A surprised silence.

STAY AWAKE

The next morning, Ms. Byrd told Clayton, "No more falling asleep in class."

"What if I can't help it?" He asked this sincerely, and not in his usual shruggy, cool manner. Clayton wasn't dumb. He knew *The Four Corners of the World* wasn't just a book; it was the bedtime book that sent him off on adventures that folded into a world of dreaming. Even when he read the book himself, he heard Cool Papa's voice. He couldn't put his sleeping in class into words, and even if he could, what would it matter? His mother would only blame Cool Papa for one more thing.

"Clayton," his mother said. "You slept eight and a half hours. That's how I know you can help it. You're too well rested to fall asleep during class."

"But sometimes I really can't help it." He hoped she believed him. He hoped she'd call him "angel" — not that he wanted to be called that all the time. He only knew his mother believed him or wanted to believe him when she thought he was her angel.

Ms. Byrd said firmly, "Tell yourself, 'I must not sleep in class. I must not sleep in class.' You'll be all right."

"But what if that doesn't work?" he asked.

"If that doesn't work, pinch yourself hard the minute you feel your eyelids drooping." She grabbed his wrists, looked him in both eyes, and said, "Now, promise me you'll stay awake."

The bus driver honked the horn and Clayton freed himself, then grabbed his book bag.

"Bye, Mom," he said quickly. But he didn't promise he'd stay awake.

"Yo, Sleepster!"

"SleepSTAH!"

It wasn't only his classmates calling him that, but everyone on the bus was doing it, too. Sleepster. He didn't hate it, but he didn't like it, either.

Ms. Treadwell smiled when he walked in

71

and placed an envelope from his mother on her desk. She didn't make a big fuss about his return, which Clayton liked.

His mother was right about being well rested, he thought. He felt alert and ready. Restless. It wasn't fun being away from things, especially if his mother stayed home with him and he couldn't play his blues harp. He'd rather be in school.

Clayton was having a fairly good school day. He sang "The Colors of the Sun" along with his class, and he solved a math problem. He volunteered to read a paragraph aloud during Social Studies, but didn't feel like helping his team advance the soccer ball in gym. Too much running. As long as he was quiet in his disobedience, he figured he was okay. Finally came lunch, and after lunch there was reading. The class was now up to chapters five and six. It didn't matter that he knew what happened in those chapters. He worried about actually reading in class and keeping his eyes open. He repeated his mother's words as he opened his book. "I must not sleep in class. I must not sleep in class."

Clayton got into the groove of reading and chanting. He found that he could read the words on the page and silently chant at the same time. It was like counting while playing the blues harp. He could do both.

He could also steal glances at the lizard when it moved, swinging its tail from side to side. Tilting his head, Clayton saw the lizard, frozen where it stood atop the rock den. The lizard shot its tongue out and then disappeared into patches of clover. That made Clayton smile. He liked that lizard.

Clayton heard pages turning around him, so he rejoined Pablo de Pablo on his journey and shortened his chant to "Stay awake, man. Stay awake."

His neighbor Alma giggled so he whispered, "Stay awake, man. Stay awake."

But the drowsy feeling was coming in waves. Small waves, like the first waves that met Pablo de Pablo and his boat. Then larger waves, crashing and pulling. Clayton's eyelids began to flutter.

"Stay awake, man. Stay awake."

Pablo de Pablo, by most measures, was a boy — and a small one at that. Rising toward him came a group of men. Small men. Smaller than he was tall. Yet still, they were men. They came by the hundreds, chanting words unfamiliar to his ears.

Clayton couldn't see them, but he could

feel them. Small men by the hundreds sur-
rounding him, dancing on his head and
latching on to his eyelids.

"No," he said aloud, and pinched himself.
Hard.

That helped. For one whole page. He had
shaken the small men off and away from
him. At least most of them.

Clayton tried. He really tried. How he
tried to stop the men from climbing down
his head and pulling him down deep into
sleep, but Cool Papa's voice in his head was
getting to the good part of the story.

Deep in his heart Pablo de Pablo feared
the small men. There were so many of
them and there was only one of him. And
then he remembered! He had the most
wonderful gift to offer, and walked boldly
to greet the throng of men.

Clayton stopped chanting altogether as he
read. He felt the words on the page lulling
him to go deeper into the adventure. His
breathing became sleep-heavy while his
body no longer fought to stay upright and
alert. His mouth slackened like a wet,
boingy rubber band, and before he could
do anything about it, his head teetered, tot-

tered. Then, *THUNK!* His forehead hit his desk.

He snorted a big snore and awakened and cried, "OW!" — each thing happening on top of the other.

His classmates roared with laughter, but his forehead smarted. When he looked up, holding his head, Ms. Treadwell stood before him, tapping her toe. It wasn't a music-loving toe-tap.

Scolding Tones

Everyone saw Clayton leave the school with his mother. Some had even laughed at him and teased him about the whipping he had coming.

Clayton wasn't worried about a whipping. His mother wasn't the whipping kind. She'd take away his treasures first, the things he loved, and the things he loved to do. But she didn't believe in whipping. She did, however, believe in scolding.

Clayton's mother scolded from the time they left the school to the time she drove home to the time they got in the house. Even when she wasn't out-and-out scolding, she spoke in scolding tones. In you-know-betters, what's-gotten-into-yous. She said over and over, "Your grandfather's passing is no excuse for this behavior."

Clayton remained silent through the scolding. He couldn't tell her what was wrong if he wanted to. He didn't understand it all himself. Even if he could tell her, she would only blame Cool Papa, and Clayton was tired of her being angry at the person he loved the most. He said nothing.

"You can't just do as you want to because you want to."

But Clayton hadn't done a thing he wanted to do. He didn't want to read the book, but he didn't want to fall asleep in class, either. He wanted to jam with his grandfather. Be with his grandfather. But his grandfather was gone. The Bluesmen were ready to hit the road again. If he did what he wanted, he'd go on the road with the Bluesmen. And the thought popped into his mind again, like it did when he sat in the pastor's office and figured things out with the Rubik's Cube. It wasn't like a fleeting idea that disappeared like waking dreams, but like something that could be real.

"You've been nothing but disruptive in class."

"I couldn't help it."

"Your teacher assigns the book to the class

but it's not the book you want to read, so you tell the teacher you don't want to read it."

"That's because I already read it."

"That's not the point, Clayton. You don't listen. You're just like your father."

That wasn't what he expected. She always said, "You're just like your grandfather," which he had always taken to be a good thing no matter how angrily she said it. But his father? Even though his mother made sure he spent one weekend out of the month with Mr. Miller, Ms. Byrd rarely spoke of him. She'd ask if they had a good time when he went on his monthly visit, and what did they eat? But that was about all.

"You can't just do what you want. Take off and go where you want. Have everything your way."

Clayton didn't answer because he didn't know who she was talking about. Him? His grandfather? Or maybe his father.

It couldn't have been him. She didn't know about his playing in Washington Square Park with Cool Papa and the Bluesmen. If she'd known, he would have heard about it in scolding tones from sunup until sundown for nearly the rest of his life.

His mother couldn't have meant his father, who'd missed one monthly visit because of a business trip. His father wasn't the "take off and go" kind. In fact, his father offered to pick Clayton up every other weekend, but Ms. Byrd always said, "Not yet."

Clayton knew exactly who she meant. Ms. Byrd was still angry with Cool Papa. He had been the one who'd taken off and gone when the sea or the road called. That's who she was mad at this time. And him. His mother was angry at him, too.

"You can't make it by following your own tune," his mother said.

Tune! Of course she meant Cool Papa Byrd. And the blues.

"I want you to succeed in this world," she said as she marched up the stairs. "And I'll do whatever it takes to make sure that happens."

Just like Clayton could read the tones and nods and ghost notes of Cool Papa's guitar-playing, he could read what it meant when her usual scolding tones changed to something more hard and firm. He knew she had come to a decision, and he was afraid of what that decision could be. He followed her, running to catch up, all the while chanting "Nomommynomommyno-mommy" the way kids plead to be spared the belt. He hadn't called her "Mommy" since he was a little kid, but "Nomommy" was all that poured out of his mouth.

She marched to his room. He was close behind her. She threw back the pillow where his silver blues harp lay. Clayton dove for it, but Ms. Byrd was faster and snatched it in one clean swipe.

"No more blues," she said, waving the silver harp. "No more of this low-down sound in this house."

She turned on her heel and took the blues harp into her room, her white marshmallow soles thumping.

The next sound he heard was a drawer slam.

A pain shot into his gut. A deep-down pain. But he didn't cry. Wouldn't cry.

THE PLAN

Clayton Byrd went to bed that night with a lot of anger, but also with a plan. He thrashed about, kicking the covers away. He was too angry to hear the music in his mind that had put him to sleep for the past two weeks since Cool Papa died. He was too angry to close his eyes to hear the sweet, sleepy melody of their last midnight jam. Clayton didn't want to imagine the sound of his blues harp. He wanted to hold his blues harp and sink it down between his lips while he savored those notes and chords. But his blues harp might as well have been an ocean away. All he could hear was the sound of a drawer slamming, over and over. So he came up with a plan as he lay in the dark.

He repeated the steps of his plan, his eyes on the window left ajar, as the sheer blue curtains swayed. Soon it would be too chilly to keep the window cracked open, but Clayton was so hot. So angry, his skin hurt. The cool air wafting into Clayton's room was a good thing. Perhaps the only good thing that night. For, along with the steps of the plan ran all the thoughts he held on to about his mother. None of them good. Not a one.

All he knew for the moment was the plan, and that she would be sorry that she had taken everything away from him. Everything that was rightfully his.

In the morning, his mother said, "I'm only doing what's best for you."

Clayton gave her a vacant look. He drank his milk, took two bites of his toast, chewed, swallowed, and stuffed the rest in his mouth.

"Keep it up," his mother said.

"Or what?" His mouth was full of toast.

She already had his blues harp. What else could she take? Clayton didn't care. Clayton had a plan.

Ms. Byrd was exhausted by Clayton. She took a moment before she spoke. "You're not a teenager yet, so stop trying my patience." She handed him an envelope. "Give this to your teacher. I can't come running to the school if you decide to fall asleep in class. There's nothing wrong with you, so stop creating problems where there are no problems. You're fine, Clayton."

He took the envelope and bent down to put it in his considerably lightened book bag. He kept the book bag at his feet, almost under the table, so his mother wouldn't notice its sunken-in shape. She would discover his textbooks, calculator, and pencil case under his bed later.

The school bus honked and Clayton said, "Bye."

Clayton and Omar boarded the bus, and the bus lurched forward. Then one voice said, "Yo, Sleepster!" And the other voices joined in. It took only one person to start things.

The driver stopped the bus.

"If I hear one more 'Sleepster' I'll turn this bus around and the troublemakers can all go back home. Let's see how you like it when you walk to school."

No one seemed worried by the driver's threat. Clayton knew the bus driver couldn't kick anyone off the bus. The last driver who had ordered a foul-mouthed kid off the bus had been fired.

Nonetheless, the noisiness quieted down. As soon as the bus driver restarted the engine, someone shouted "Sleepster!" in a high-pitched, funny voice. Even Clayton laughed. Then, for the rest of the ride, the rowdier kids snored loudly. Clayton joined them.

Omar slugged him in the shoulder, the way friends do.

The bus pulled up to the front of the school, taking its place behind a line of unloading school buses. Clayton, Omar, and the other kids got off the bus to join the mob of kids waiting to enter the building. Clayton and Omar neared the entrance.

"Dang. No pen."

"Take one of mine," Omar offered.

"That's all right, man," Clayton said. "I'll run across the street. Pick one up."

"You'll be late."

"I'll run fast," Clayton said, and took off toward the bodega. Once inside, he stood near the door and watched Omar disappear into the school. He went to the counter and said, "MetroCard," as cool as he could. He put his ten-dollar bill, his cut from playing with Cool Papa and the Bluesmen, on the counter. The store clerk, who didn't give

Clayton a second glance, smacked a Metro-Card down on the counter.

It was seven forty-five and the plan was in action. Clayton avoided the main streets and began the three-quarter-mile hike to his house. His mother should have been on her way to work, creeping along on the expressway in her car.

Still, Clayton took a deep, careful breath when he turned the corner onto his block. He saw what he expected to see. An empty driveway. He exhaled, ran to the side door, let himself in with his key, and ran up the stairs. So far, so good.

He opened his mother's bedroom door carefully, as if she might still be there. But he was alone. And now, to find his blues harp.

He opened drawer after drawer of her highboy. Six drawers of silky things. Underthings that belonged to his mother. It was when he pulled open the highest drawer that he knew. He should have known to begin with! The highest drawer was a hiding drawer to keep something away from a kid. But though Clayton was a kid, he was tall enough to get what he needed from the top drawer without having to stand on anything. He was sure he'd be able to look his mother straight in the eye in another year. After all, his mother wasn't growing any taller, but he could feel himself inching up.

His hand found the candy-bar-shaped metal instantly. He wiped it clean of the silky, girly things it had been smothered by, and then sank it in his mouth to slick it up. Then he blew into all the holes, sliding upward, and drew in the air to slide back down.

He went inside his room, opened the closet, and grabbed the porkpie hat. He took the rest of his money — seventeen dollars in bills — folded them, and zipped up the cash in his book bag. He ran down the stairs, threw a peanut butter cracker snack into the nearly empty book bag, tucked his MetroCard in his pants pocket, stuffed his silver blues harp in his jacket pocket, and put the porkpie hat on his head.

He was about to run out the back door, but he stopped. Turned. Walked to the dining room table. Picked up the glass salt-shaker. The angel with the glued-on wing. He put it on the floor, raised his right foot, and smashed it.

Then he left.

CLAYTON BYRD GOES UNDERGROUND

Clayton trotted happily, sneakily, down the concrete and steel steps of the subway station. He paid his fare, pushed his slim body against the turnstile bar, and embarked on his adventure. He chuckled to himself. Glee wasn't a song from Ms. Treadwell's *Great American Book of Glee.* Glee was being on the lam, making a great escape. Each level of steps in Clayton's descent took him farther below street level until Clayton Byrd was truly underground.

He had never noticed the grunge of the platform before, when he and Cool Papa snuck off to the city to meet up with the Bluesmen on double-shift nights. He was just as blind to it all now as he stood alone.

The smoke-dulled wall tiles, the over-spilling garbage cans, the blackened, gummy ground, and the stale air were not enough to warn him away. He didn't notice the grime and dirt, or the long, brawny rats running across the track — he was too elated by the success of his plan.

The details of what was to follow were hazy at best. Details such as food, drink, a change of clothing, a place to sleep, and needing more than the seventeen dollars squirreled away in the zipper pouch of his book bag. All of those details would work themselves out when he caught up with the Bluesmen.

By Clayton's calculation, this was the last week that he'd be able to find the Bluesmen in Washington Square Park before they headed south. He'd never been to the South, but he knew the Bluesmen preferred the southern climate to the cold that would soon drape over New York.

Even though he was a kid, the Bluesmen had treated Clayton like a musician. Like a bluesman, although he was still growing into his spot with the band. He knew their rhythms and patterns. He'd play off of their riffs and not on top of them, unless they played a tidal wave of chords where everyone jammed together. He would wait to be waved in and not whine or plead for a solo. He was at his best when he saw himself as a musician. A bluesman.

A woman's figure entered his periphery. He felt the heat of her stare on his cheek. If he walked away she'd know he didn't belong underground. He rocked on his heels and waited for the train.

At the other end of the platform stood some boys. Two older. The other two not. He didn't turn his head to look at them. He knew better than to turn and gawk. Instead, he positioned himself so he could see who was on one end of the platform and who was on the other.

They looked wild. Feral. Definitely not like they were on their way to school, but more like fighting wolf pups, batting and nipping at one another for exercise, especially the younger two. At a glance, those two looked like twins. Though it seemed friendly between them, Clayton knew that didn't mean they'd want him staring at them.

He saw the tallest boy among them hold his hand up. The others stopped clowning or play-fighting and quieted themselves. The tall one stood at the edge of the platform and cocked his ear toward the tracks.

"Train!" he shouted.

Clayton stepped closer toward the platform's edge to peer down the tunnel. He saw no lights and heard no rumble.

The boys ran to the very end of the platform and seemed to wait.

Then, Clayton heard the train rumble. Within seconds he saw two bright lights barreling out of the dark.

When the silver subway train roared into the station, the car before him opened and he stepped inside, found a seat, and looked dreamily ahead while the car took him on his adventure.

The hard-staring woman took the seat directly across from him.

"Look sharp. Be cool," Cool Papa used to tell him when they were on the train heading toward the city. He took those words now as if Cool Papa was there beside him keeping his secret. He cocked his head and looked sharp so no one would see a boy on the lam, and would instead see a bluesman on the way to his gig. *Gig.* A Cool Papa word. If he looked like a bluesman on his way to some place in particular, no one would look at him the way the lady on the platform, now sitting before him, did.

If only he had shades.

Clayton did have his blues harp, and that was the main thing. A bluesman without an ax was just a man riding the train. And a kid without his ax couldn't claim to be a bluesman. *Ax.* Another Cool Papa word. He had his ax, or what Jack Rabbit Jones had called his "union card." The way he worked on those square holes, he might as well be chopping wood. One day he'd get that blues bend just right. He'd make that harp start from a deep place, then turn around the corner until that bent note came up crying. He could feel it. He was that close.

And he had Cool Papa Byrd's porkpie hat. He set it low on his head. When he took it off, he could smell Cool Papa's scent in the headband.

The hard-staring woman didn't exactly shake her head, but Clayton could feel she wanted to. He stared past her, when he felt like getting up, walking up to her, and asking her to please lean away so he could get a good look at the subway map. That would only invite questions. *Where are you going? Shouldn't you be in school? Boy, where is your mama?*

He stared off. Better to not give himself away.

The subway pulled into the next station and the doors flew open.

A smell — foul, sweet, and funky — caught his nose. His nostrils closed faster on their own than he could have told them to. A woman in rags pushed through the moving train with her shopping cart of treasures. She was a mound of soiled clothes, surrounded by knotted plastic bags, bundled newspapers, and a falling-apart suitcase, stuffed with who knows what. She unloaded herself down into the corner seat of the train way over on the far end of the car and her smell kicked like two mules. That was a lyric from one of Cool Papa Byrd's blues songs.

"You kicked me, baby, worse than two mules can kick a man when he's down."

He hadn't paid much attention to the part about two mules kicking when he clamped down on his blues harp and played while Cool Papa sang those words, but when the woman's funk caught him, he knew what it was to be kicked worse than two mules kicked. He covered his nose, but not his ears.

She was singing. First he thought she was saying something. Talking to no one, the way fidgety, homeless people do. Then he heard a familiar sound. A tone and rhythm. It was a church rhythm, wrapped up in the blues.

He was tapping before he knew he was tapping. Nodding before he knew he was nodding.

"It's gonna be all right. . . ." the woman moaned. "It's gonna be all right."

Clayton would give an "amen" to that, if he were the amen type. But he agreed with the bad-smelling woman. It was going to be all right. He almost reached for his blues harp but let it stay in his pocket.

What if Cool Papa sent the hard-staring woman to let him know he still had his eye on him? What if Cool Papa sent the bad-smelling woman to let him know it would be all right? He wondered if spirits jumped from body to body because their old body was in the ground. Clayton didn't know for sure, but sitting in the train with one woman across from him and another at the other end of the car, he didn't rule out the possibility.

Every Rider, Clap Your Hands

If Cool Papa was talking to Clayton through the homeless woman, his spirit had vacated her now slumped-over body. Once her bluesy church song turned to snoring, her funky odor intensified, mule-kicking Clayton in the nose and gut full-on. Holding his hand over his nose was no longer enough.

Clayton coughed hard, then sprang out of his seat. The car bounced and jerked as he made his way over to the other end of the car to escape the woman's strong odor. He coughed again, swallowed some air, and coughed harder.

He had to get out of the car.

He read the sign plastered to the window

of the connecting car door. *Riding or moving between cars is prohibited.* The circled image of a person standing between two train cars with a red slash running through the circle was equally clear. Still, he ignored the warnings. Clayton pulled down on the metal door handle and yanked the door open. He found himself between the two cars, the train bouncing violently. He wiped his eyes, teary from the coughing fit, and lingered for a few seconds on the narrow outer ledge of the subway car. He kept one hand on the door handle, the other on Cool Papa's porkpie hat. He couldn't let his hat get away from him, and the train was moving fast. The stale smoky air was better than the air he'd escaped from. Finally he pushed the door open.

Clayton's sneakers hugged the shaky floor as he made his way from pole to pole. He stopped at the subway map. No one sat in the seat just below the map, so he leaned in to get a good look, and counted the number of stops before he'd reach West Fourth Street station. Now that where he was going was firm in his mind, he slid into the empty seat below the posted subway map. He counted fifteen station stops. It would be a long ride.

He stared out into the tunnel where graffiti tags passed by. *HARD KNOX. LYFER. CRY* in puffy white-cloud letters.

He wished he had something to read. Anything to read — except for *The Four Corners of the World.* He couldn't afford to fall asleep on the train. All that was left to stare at was the subway floor, or across the train, or up at the business school ads posted above him. He didn't want to get caught staring at any of the riders, because people were touchy about being stared at. From quick glances he allowed himself, all he saw were dull, empty faces. People reading or absorbed by the music piped in through earphones. The train seemed to move slowly, but that was okay. Soon he'd be with Jack Rabbit Jones, Big Mike, and Hector Santos. People who knew Cool Papa as a bluesman, and knew him as Clayton Byrd on blues harp. He couldn't get there soon enough.

The train pulled into a stop. Its bell rang, *ding-dong-ding,* and the doors opened. People rushed on, and the recorded conductor's voice said, "Stand clear of the closing doors, please." The train bell rang again, *ding-dong-ding,* and began to close, but a tall kid in a dirty white tank top jumped into the car, wedging himself between the closing doors, and shouted, "Jump on! Jump on!"

Train Ear! Clayton thought. The kid on the platform.

Next, a boy wearing a fuzzy white Kangol cap, who was slightly younger and shorter than Train Ear but definitely older than the twins, squeezed himself past the lanky teen and into the car.

The sliding doors clamped in on Train Ear a couple times, but he stayed in the doorway and shouted, "Come on! Come on!" while the voice over the loudspeaker said, "Stand clear of the closing doors, please," and the passengers groaned.

Finally, Train Ear pulled in the last of their pack. A boy about Clayton's height and age, maybe a year older, carrying a boom box, and then, that boy's twin, who carried nothing. Once all were inside the car and out of the way of the closing doors, the doors opened and closed twice, and the train was off, the boys hooting and laughing at one another.

He glanced at the pack. They were positioned in the center of the car and at the center doors on both sides of the car. He glanced, was careful not to stare. The little bit that he saw told him what he needed to know. Their sneakers were all nearly new, although their T-shirts and jeans were ripped and grungy. One wore a white hat. Clayton was no fool. Those sneakers had been stolen. Wherever those boys were from, it wasn't the same place that he came from. There was no one to see to it that their clothes were clean, heads were shaved around the edges, skin was oiled and not ashy. They were not the kind his mother would let sit at her table with dirty hands to handle her salt and pepper shaker angels. Well, the pepper angel.

Wolf pack, Clayton thought.

He wanted to look away but couldn't. He needed a book. Something to keep him from staring. But he had the sense that the wolf pack was there to do something. They were loud, both begging and daring people to look their way.

One twin sat the boom box on the ground and clicked the dial. The little bit of sound that crackled through its speakers moaned and died out. The boom-box boy shook the dead box, and slapped it on the sides a couple of times. "Oh well" was all he had to say.

"I told you, snatch some batteries!" Train Ear yelled at him.

Boom Box shrank-shrugged.

Train Ear yelled to Boom Box's twin,

"Step up!"

The twin jumped out into the center of the train car and made noise. Deep sounds from the inside of his throat, through his nose, lips, and teeth. The boy was a human beatbox.

Train Ear shouted at the people on the train,

"EVERY RIDER, CLAP YOUR HANDS —
YOU HEARD ME —
TRAIN RIDERS, CLAP YOUR HANDS! —
I KNOW YOU HEARD ME —
TRAIN RIDERS, CLAP YOUR HANDS!"

But the people on the train read their newspapers, continued their conversations, or stared out into the dark tunnel.

Only the twins and the boy with the white cap clapped their hands. Yet before he knew it, Clayton's foot tapped to the hip-hop beat, a simple rhythm with the clap on the first and third beat. It was easy to fall in.

The grunting twin, "Beat Box," was close. So close, Clayton caught his spit a few times as he beatboxed. Clayton liked the sounds and didn't mind the spit. He could almost feel the vibrations of the grunts that thumped and strummed like a bass. He liked the grunting that belched deep from

Boom Box's gut like a tom-tom. He followed how the boy clicked his tongue like a snare, and timed his crisp hisses like sticks on brass hi-hats.

Clayton liked the sounds and the beats, but he missed chords. He missed the melody.

Without thinking twice, Clayton took his harp from his pocket, found a spot, and came in with the beat, but not on top of the beat.

Boom Box said, "Oh, wow!" But Beat Box turned to Clayton. Nodded at him, without breaking the rhythm. He'd say something through his self-made bass, drums, and crisp hi-hats, and Clayton spoke back with his harp. Beat Box would start a phrase, and Clayton would jump into the phrase with an answer. Then they began to talk. Really talk. How Clayton missed that. Needed that.

Beat Box lowered his volume but kept the beat. He nodded to Clayton, who didn't have to be told he was being waved in for a solo. Twelve bars.

A few hands applauded.

Show Your Love

"Check it," Beat Box said to Clayton. "Step with us. Like this." He, Boom Box, and the older kid with the fuzzy white Kangol cap stepped to the left, then slid-hopped and stepped to the right.

"Get up," Boom Box told him.

Clayton got out of his seat and went to the end of their line. He bobbed first, the way he did when he kept the groove with the Bluesmen. The beat was simple enough, but he didn't try the slide-hopping. Instead, he came in with his left foot, bobbed, then the right foot. The slide-hopping in between would work itself out eventually.

Now that there was rhythm and music,

Train Ear began the show. They were on the longest ride between stations. It was plenty enough time to put on a show.

Train Ear ran down the aisle and swung himself around the pole. His legs whirligigged like blades, then they clamped around the pole, and he held up his hands to suspend himself like Spiderman. He grabbed the pole, lifted his feet up over his head, against the pole, and climbed down using his hands, until his palms were flat on the ground. With knees bent and both feet still above his head, Train Ear "hand-walked" backward and then forward, his sneakers just missing the faces and newspapers of a few riders. The train jerked and he kicked a woman's book out of her hands. She picked her book up and continued to read, never once looking up.

Those who looked on did so with mild fear, disgust, or boredom. No one was as impressed as Clayton. He had seen guys dancing on the train or on the street before, but he was never this close — and had never been in it.

For most of the riders, it was one dance exhibition too many.

"Show your love!" shouted the teen with the fuzzy white cap. "Show your love!" he said as he ran up and down the aisle with his cap out. Riders mostly looked away, kept their noses in books and newspapers. A few looked stiffly into the boy's almost pleading face and just said, "No."

There was no love for Train Ear.

As he stepped back with the line, the teen trying to collect money walked, or rolled, to the center of the car. To Clayton, it looked like he rolled, because his feet seemed to not leave the train floor. Everything about him was fluid. He didn't jump out at the people, like Train Ear did. Instead, he kept himself to a small space, but seemed to make big, amazing things happen, like jump roping over his own arm. It was as if he had no skeleton at all.

"Man! Did you see that?" Clayton said. "He's got bones like jelly!"

Beat Box knocked Clayton in the shoulder the way Clayton would have knocked Omar. "It's showtime. Blow."

Clayton kept blowing and drawing in breath on his blues harp to the beat, but wondered what Omar was doing. If Omar looked for him during gym or in the lunchroom or if he'd try to hold a seat for him on the bus. His thoughts of Omar and school popped in and then out.

"Jelly Bones" craned his neck like an Egyptian robot: his feet went left, arms in *s*'s, snaking left and right. He collapsed down to the ground, and wound his body upward like a cobra.

Clayton caught on quickly and blew the snake-charmer tune. The lady who had dropped her book tried not to smile. But her toe tapped.

Train Ear shouted, "Let's hear it for my man!" The boys all hooted. And a few hands actually clapped.

This time, when Jelly Bones walked the aisle with his fuzzy white cap, a few riders dropped in a dollar bill here and there, and some coins.

Boom Box leapfrogged over his twin, jumping to the dance spot.

Something had changed.

Clayton felt it without looking to see what it was. It felt familiar. He knew exactly what it was. The love. Not the all-out love the people in the park had for Cool Papa Byrd and the Bluesmen. No one was going to shout "Do that dance, boy!" like they shouted "Play that thang!" to Cool Papa and the Bluesmen. But some of the annoyed, frightened, or unaffected faces now wore thin smiles.

Clayton enjoyed playing to the beat. Or between the beats. He kept his ears open to answer Beat Box, and he kept his eyes on

Boom Box, to give him notes to dance on.

This dance was different. It wasn't just steps and moves. Boom Box was telling a story. First, he ran a bunch of steps in place. With the jerking of the train, it seemed like he was running a race, his arms pumping, his knees hitting his chest, the train chugging. He looked over his right shoulder and then his left shoulder, like he was being chased. Then he ran in slow motion. He twisted his lips and bugged out his eyes in a mask of fear. He threw both hands up in the air, and stopped, like someone had shouted, "FREEZE!" But his motions went back to running a race, a million steps in place. And his chest went *pop-lock, pop* and *lock, pop*! And he fell to the ground. He crawled, reaching out to the pointed heel of one sitting lady, and mimed the word *Help.* Then he rolled onto his back, two legs up, then down. He was stiff and laid out.

The boys marched around his laid-out body — with Clayton lagging behind, not sure what to do. On "one," they bent down. On "two," they grabbed the "dead" dancer and hoisted him up. Then they walked a slow, stiff march, like he was in a coffin and they were his pallbearers.

Clayton played the death march. The one he heard on cartoons and at the end of old video games. But he kept the one and three hip-hop beat on the tune. Jelly Bones took off his fuzzy white cap out of respect for "the departed." They marched slowly down the narrow train aisle, Jelly Bones holding out his cap to anyone who cared to throw in coins or a dollar.

And then a man stuck a five-dollar bill at Clayton.

Clayton almost stopped. He nodded to the man and took the five, letting his eyes smile, since his mouth was engaged in blowing and drawing. He passed the five to Train Ear, marched behind the others, and kept playing.

BEAT BOYS

The train pulled into the next station. Just as the train came to a complete stop, Train Ear shouted, "Beats out!" The "dead" boy came to life, ran and grabbed the boom box, and they began to crowd and push out of the opening train doors. Except for Clayton, who'd gone back to his seat.

As the people rushed in, Train Ear stuck his head inside the car and yelled, "YO!" to Clayton.

Clayton didn't move.

Train Ear shouted, "YO! YOU! Get off! Get off! Come on!"

Beat Box, Boom Box, and Jelly Bones waved their arms and shouted at him. "Come on! Come on!"

Ding-dong-ding. "Stand clear of the closing doors, please." *Ding-dong-ding.*

Clayton didn't think. He got up and ran to the closing door, and then Train Ear, who blocked the doors with his skinny body, pulled him off the train.

Ding-dong-ding. "Stand clear of the closing doors, please."

Clayton stood on the train platform, surrounded by Train Ear and the three boys. He'd given Train Ear the five-dollar bill. What more did they want?

"Who you?" Train Ear asked.

Clayton didn't want to blink but he did. "Clayton," he said. *Look sharp. Be cool.* "Byrd."

Beat Box started cawing, and the other boys joined in. "Caw! Caw! Caw!" They were so loud and crazy with their cawing and flapping, he knew what it meant to be surrounded by a murder of crows.

"So show us what you got, Clay Bird," the tallest teen said. "What's in the bag?"

Before Clayton could open his mouth, Jelly Bones and Boom Box grabbed the straps of his book bag and yanked it off his shoulders.

"Hey!" Clayton said.

"It's light," Jelly Bones said, giving it a shake before he tossed the blue bag to Train Ear.

"No diggity," Train Ear said. He shook the bag and tore open the zippers. Seventeen dollars. Now his. A peanut butter and cracker snack. He squeezed the little pack until the crackers crumbled and threw the orangey mush back in the bag.

"Don't you have school or something?" Train Ear asked. "Where's your books?"

"Who are you? My mama or something?" Clayton said this knowing his mother was a "mother" and not a "mama."

"Oh! Caw! Caw! Caw!" the others said.

"Your mama! He said you his mama!" Beat Box said.

Look sharp. Be cool. Don't smile, he added to himself.

Train Ear wasn't cool, although he tried to play it off. He threw the book bag at Clayton's feet, and when Clayton bent down to scoop it up, Train Ear swiped his hat, when he was tall enough to just take it.

"Now I'm your pops," Train Ear said, putting Cool Papa's hat on his head.

"Hey," Clayton said again. "That's mine." He knew he had no chance of getting his money back, but the hat was altogether different.

"Don't worry, Clay Bird. I'll give it back when I'm done." Train Ear grinned. His face was roughly cut. What Cool Papa would have described as "hard pretty." He seemed to like the hat.

Clayton said, "All right," even though it wasn't all right. It wasn't all right that the dude who probably hadn't washed his thickly packed and matted hair in a month was killing the last of Cool Papa Byrd's smell with his sweated-up head.

"So what was that you were playing?" Train Ear asked. "A harmonica or something?"

Clayton took the harmonica out of his pocket. A mistake, but he showed it anyway. "It's a blues harp, man," Clayton said. Cool Papa never called it a harmonica, although sometimes he called it a Mississippi saxophone. Clayton couldn't see himself telling the tall, scary dancer that fact.

"Blow something, *man,*" Jelly Bones said, mocking the way Clayton said "man," which was Cool Papa's way of saying "man." "Make some noise!"

Then the three boys — but not Train Ear — clapped their hands and did their hip-hop sliding step. One — cross left, then two — cross right. It wasn't a blues beat. He couldn't show them what he, Clayton Byrd on blues harp, really had to say, but he could play with the rhythm and speak their language. So he raised his blues harp to his lips to blow, but Train Ear snatched the silver bar from his hands.

The three seemed to stop in mid-time-step. They looked up at Train Ear. "Whatcha doing?" Beat Box asked.

"Hey, man!" Clayton said, reaching out for the harp. "That's mine."

"No, Clay Bird," Train Ear said. "It's mine now."

"Then play it," Clayton said.

The three boys echoed, "Play it, play it, play it," until Train Ear raised it to his mouth and blew. Hard. A high-pitched shriek ripped into the air. Another blow produced a squeal. He blew harder.

The boys laughed, although they didn't know what Clayton knew. That Train Ear was holding the blues harp with the wrong side up. After Clayton had made his first squeaks, Cool Papa showed him the tricks to knowing which side was up: Make sure the round bolts that welded the blues harp together were on top and not the square bolts. And that the numbers one through ten were always on the top side.

Train Ear held the blues harp aloft, ready to throw it onto the tracks.

"Wait!" Clayton said.

"Why, Clay Bird?" Train Ear said. "Why should I wait?" He stepped closer to the

111

edge of the platform, his arm in pitching motion.

On the inside Clayton choked. Everything he felt, everything his blues harp was to him, was coiled around his rapid breathing. The thumping in his head. His hot red ears.

"Because," Beat Box said, "he keeps the beat."

"He makes some NOISE!" Boom Box said.

"We got paid," Jelly Bones said. "They," he said of the train riders, "like his playing."

The others agreed. Clayton kept a beat and he made the right kind of noise.

Clayton heard Cool Papa. *Look sharp. Be cool.* He shrugged and said, "It's the only one I got."

"Come on, man," Beat Box said.

"Come on," the others said. "Give it back."

Train Ear laughed. "Okay, Clay Bird. But you have to answer this one question."

"Shoot," Clayton said. Furthermore, he didn't want to be called Clay Bird — and from the way the boys cawed, he knew they saw a "bird." Not a Byrd. He didn't have his blues harp in his hand or in his pocket so he kept that observation to himself.

"We're the Beat Boys," Train Ear said.

"Beat Boys!" echoed around him.

"MAKING NOISE —
TO THEM, WE'RE INVISIBLE —
MAKING NOISE —
TO US, WE'RE INDIVISIBLE!"

"So, are you down with us, Clay Bird?"

Clayton looked up at his blues harp. His grandfather's porkpie hat.

"Down with us?" Beat Box asked.

"Or get beat down?" Train Ear asked.

Clayton was certain Train Ear would throw his blues harp onto the train tracks, but within him, he also knew the other Beat Boys wouldn't give him a beatdown.

But then Train Ear cocked his head. Tossed the blues harp to Clayton, who didn't expect it, but caught it.

"Nice catch," Beat Box said, his eyes fixed on the blues harp. To Clayton, Beat Box seemed a little embarrassed, like he had been caught wanting something he couldn't have. "Show me how to play that," Beat Box both said and asked.

Clayton shrugged, as if to say okay. *But not right now,* he told himself. He had just gotten his blues harp back, and he wasn't ready to let go of it.

"A stop away," Train Ear said, his voice different. Not teasing and threatening. Serious. "Showtime."

Clayton pressed his ear to the air but couldn't hear the oncoming rumble. He stuck his blues harp in his pocket and followed the Beat Boys to the other end of the platform.

The Opposite of Bluesman

They like his playing. That was what Jelly
Bones said. But what did that matter without his hat? He eyed the porkpie hat tilted
on Train Ear's squirrely head. Cool Papa's
words came back to him. *I'm not raising you
to be some cute kid.* Those words were funny
back then. *Cute kid.* But now he could see
Cool Papa's face and hear disgust in the
hard K sounds. *Cute kid.* The opposite of a
bluesman.

Clayton rubbed his hands. A prickly feeling jumped to his ears. And then to his
cheeks. He rubbed all over.

Beat Box tapped him. "What's wrong with
you?"

115

Boom Box said, "Bedbugs."

"I don't have no bedbugs, man," Clayton said. Just a feeling he couldn't put into words, but a face he could see. Disgust he could hear, as if Cool Papa looked down on him from wherever he was. *Is that who you are? A snake charmer? A cute kid blowing a harmonica, making the people smile?* And his grandfather never called the blues harp a harmonica. Never.

"Clay Bird's one weird bird," Boom Box said.

"But he gets them tapping," Jelly Bones said. "And dropping change."

Train Ear nodded. "He's down with us. He's ours. Right, Clay Bird?"

"My hat, man," Clayton said.

They only laughed. Except Beat Box. He didn't laugh.

Headlights like bright eyes came around the dark bending tunnel. A train, to take him farther away from his plan. And yet, when the train pulled in, and the doors slid open, and the prickly feeling jumped to his knee, Clayton followed Beat Box, Boom Box, Jelly Bones, Train Ear — and Cool Papa's porkpie hat — into the train car.

He pulled his harp out of his pants pocket and wiped Train Ear's spit and fingerprints off its body. To be sure, he wiped it again before sinking the blues harp deep into his mouth. He hated Train Ear. Hated him. And yet when it was time to play his part, he pulled air from deep down and blew.

Train Ear's arms were so long, he almost hit a man. That didn't stop him from spreading his skinny arms wide and shouting, "EVERY RIDER, CLAP YOUR HANDS!"

While the others shouted, "YOU HEARD HIM!"

"EVERY RIDER, CLAP YOUR HANDS!"

The Beats had scrambled to their posts, which wasn't easy, since the train car was occupied. Every seat filled, every pole leaned on or clung to. The center of the train, the spot where Train Ear would do his backflips, pole spins, and whirligig legs, was already occupied by a man wearing a broken-down top hat and a once-black cape, and holding a wand. The magician had tapped the wand three times and was about to say "Abracadabra!" or whatever Clayton imagined magicians say as they pulled off their magic trick. But between the chanting, the harp chords, and the train rumble, the magician was losing his audience.

The magician's already sagging, ruddy

face reddened even more. He was a sorry-looking guy. However, sorry didn't stop him from shouting "MOVE IT, FELLAS! MOVE IT!" at Train Ear and the boys. "I'm working here. I'm working."

Train Ear shouted back, "THIS IS OUR TRAIN!" and the boys, except for Clayton, joined him:

"WE RUN THIS TRAIN —
WE ROCK THIS TRAIN —
YOU BETTER SIT DOWN —
OR GET BEAT DOWN!"

Train Ear moved toward the magician. "You beat it or get beat down. You heard me."

Clayton didn't want any part of getting or giving a beatdown. He hoped the Beats' words were all rhythm. Just talk that sounded good. But now Train Ear was face-to-face with the magician.

"You're ruining my trick!" Spit flew out of the magician's mouth as he spoke. "I had it all set up." More spit.

"Pops, did you spit on me? Did you just spit on me?" Train Ear wiped his face and pushed the magician back a step. The boys, except for Clayton, laughed. The riders who were looking on mostly shook their heads, but did and said nothing.

Clayton waited for the magician to do something. With his cape. Or the wand. Maybe throw the hat like a kung fu weapon. But the hat was too sad. Still, Clayton waited. As did most of the train riders.

The train pulled into the station.

Ding-dong-ding. "Stand clear of the closing doors, please."

The people were leaving. Those who had watched the magician's show before it came to a stop in mid-trick. The magician picked up a black case that he'd left on the floor and chased down departing train riders with his floppy top hat.

Train Ear forgot about the magician. His head snapped left. He waved his hand in an urgent circular motion. "BEATS!" And just like that, everyone ran.

Clayton didn't know what was happening or what to do. He turned and saw the policeman who entered the car, and then saw Train Ear and Cool Papa's hat taking off. Without thinking, he ran in the direction of his grandfather's hat.

Six Rings

We don't need you. We're just fine.

This is what Ms. Byrd told herself when the phone rang.

Albert Miller called the employee lounge either during lunch or during dinnertime on double-shift nights. Six rings followed by no ringing for thirty seconds. Then another six rings. It became a running joke among her coworkers. "How many rings before she gets up to answer?" One particular coworker didn't find the pleading rings amusing. Eventually, she marched over to the telephone, picked it up, spoke to the caller, and then held out the receiver to Ms. Byrd. "It's for you."

As always, Ms. Byrd stopped eating, wiped her mouth with her napkin, glared at her coworker, and took the telephone.

"Yes, Albert."

Each week Ms. Byrd and Mr. Miller had the same conversation. He either had tickets to the planetarium, the train show, or the game at the stadium. He could swing by and pick them both up — she and Clayton. She, who, unbeknownst to Clayton, loved watching a baseball game at the stadium, was always welcome to join them. They could eat hot dogs, do the seventh-inning wave. See themselves on the Jumbotron. This miraculous season, their team had made it to the postseason. "You can't miss that," Mr. Miller said hopefully.

Ms. Byrd always had a good reason why they couldn't go. This time, it was that she had just got Clayton back on track with his schoolwork. An outing of fun would send the wrong message.

She was so pleased with herself for being firm, when her best childhood memories were the few times her father was home from being out to sea or on the road. She sat between her mother and father at the baseball stadium and she munched on Cracker Jack and watched the game. When the organ played baseball songs, Papa, Mama, and Little Miss Byrd sang along.

While Mr. Miller talked, she smiled. She remembered years ago how she had treated herself to a game at the stadium, and that she had ticket number six in the center section over home plate, row B, next to seat seven. His seat. Albert Miller's.

She caught herself smiling. So did the coworker who had handed her the phone. Ms. Byrd stopped smiling.

"No, Albert. This weekend isn't good. I finally have Clayton focused. . . . No," she repeated. "A fun outing would ruin the schedule."

And he said, like he always said, "You both need me. I wish you would let me be a bigger part of his life. You need help with him."

She tried to keep her voice polite. Firm and low was the best she could do. "We're fine, Albert. I have everything under control. Clayton's fine. Just fine."

Chasing the Beats

Clayton stepped onto the subway platform, a fast- and slow-moving jigsaw puzzle with live pieces entering, exiting, milling, and turning. He made out the Beats running up ahead. He tried to catch them, but the people around him moved like zombies. Both the platform and the throng of people seemed to go on without end. He lost sight of Cool Papa's hat, but he spotted Beat Box, about three hundred feet away, waving to him frantically.

Clayton jumped high to be seen, and waved back, then dashed in Beat Box's direction. A woman pushed her stroller in the very spot where Clayton's foot landed and Clayton bumped into it. Little arms inside the stroller flew up.

"Sorry!" Clayton said.

"Boy, you better watch where you're going!" The woman stood eye to eye with Clayton, but he could see she was no one to mess with. "You kids better stop playing around."

"Sorry!" he repeated, but he kept running.

How could he watch where he was going if he didn't know where he was going? He was just running. Chasing the Beats.

"Come on! Come on!"

Clayton saw Beat Box up ahead. And then, he didn't. Beat Box had somehow disappeared into darkness.

Clayton looked to see who was behind him. Far off at the other end of the platform, he saw the navy blue of an officer's uniform. He wondered if the officer had seen Beat Box disappear. Or if the officer could see him.

He couldn't lose his hat. It was the last thing left of Cool Papa.

Without thinking, Clayton ran to the very end of the platform, pushed past the red sign that said *PROHIBITED: DO NOT ENTER,* and trotted down concrete steps until he found himself in the gray-black of the tunnel, at track level.

Clayton was now farther underground than he had ever been. With the aid of a few bald lightbulbs that hung a ways down, he made out figures running. Beat Box and the others, he thought. So he stayed close to the wall, and ran down the dusty, foot-wide walkway that jutted out merely inches from the outer rail.

Once, from a seat on a slow-moving train, Clayton had seen subway workers standing on the walkway carrying lanterns while repairing the tracks. But now he was on the slim walkway, inches from trains soon to come hurtling down the tracks.

He ran faster.

He tried to keep his ears open for sounds. Maybe a police officer behind him, or an oncoming local train. And then what? He didn't know. Maybe he'd have to flatten his back against the tunnel's wall.

Keep running, he told himself. *Catch the Beats. Catch the Beats. Get Cool Papa's hat back. Find the Bluesmen. Go on the road.*

Clayton had never run so much and so hard in his life. He found himself huffing, his lungs thinning and burning within him, his chest hurting. But his legs kept going. His nearly empty book bag was light, but his arms and legs grew heavy. Clayton wasn't much of a runner but the thought of a train or a cop on his tail turned him into a sprinter.

His inner ears felt numb. He couldn't hear any sounds up ahead. But he heard a clink. A metal-on-metal clink. His blues harp! It had slipped out of his pocket, flown a few feet ahead, and disappeared into the dark.

"Man!" Clayton's heart flopped inside his chest. Flopped and fell. Where did the harp go? He had to get it. Where was it? WHERE?

He felt his brain pinging up, down, left, right, inside his skull. He covered his head and ears and circled around and around in a small spot, but he was only making himself dizzy.

Then Clayton stopped. Stopped circling. Stopped panting. Stopped his thoughts from racing, his brain from pinging. He stood along the edge of the walkway, looking out into the dark. When he calmed down, he heard the metal-on-metal clink in his head.

The train rail! But where?

He took a few steps. The sound of the harp hitting metal had been more near than far. He kneeled. *There!* The gleam in the dark! Not on the rail or out on the tracks, like the clinking suggested, but down along the outer edge where the rectangular wooden train track ends were spaced like flat brown teeth. All wasn't lost. He could reach it. *Just kneel. Reach. Swipe.*

But as he knelt, he felt a stirring through his hands, knees, and belly. Sound. Vibration. The rumble of the oncoming train. Still, he couldn't see the glow of light that signaled the arriving train, or see headlights of the actual train. He didn't have Train Ear's gift. A gift that would buy him time. He couldn't tell if the train was an express, coming from the center track, or a local train, which would roar inches away from him. But he could feel a breeze and hear the rumble, which meant the train was near. Time was running out. The train was coming. Clayton could only imagine his harp smashed up on the train tracks.

"Man, man, man, oh man." That was as close to prayer as he could offer.

He looked behind him, in the direction of the local track. The glow in the dark drew brighter. The harp was right there. *Right there.* He leaned and reached down.

His life didn't pass before him, but his day did. The day he was supposed to have. Getting on the school bus. Singing "This Land Is Your Land." Tapping on the lizard's cage. Getting his math homework checked off. Gym. Eating cafeteria tacos. Reading *The Four Corners of the World.* One hundred men pulling his eyelids down, his head sinking onto his desk. His mother's utter disappointment.

And the day he did have: Emptying his book bag. Tricking Omar. Spending the last money his grandfather gave him. Stealing the blues harp. Smashing the glass saltshaker angel. Sneaking down into the tunnel. Chasing the Beats.

His hand found the faint silver gleam in the dark; he snatched it up, and then he rolled back against the tunnel wall.

Ten seconds later, the local train flew by him.

Clayton heard steps coming toward him. They were light steps.

"Yo, Clay Bird. Come on! Come on!"

It was Beat Box.

Clayton got up. He was dusty and dirty. He stuffed his blues harp deep into his pocket.

He ran toward Beat Box's voice and finally saw him.

"What were you doing down there?" Beat Box asked.

"Dropped my harp," Clayton said.

Beat Box shook his head. "Thought we lost you. Come on."

Clayton followed.

"That was dumb," Beat Box said. "Don't you know about the third rail? Fry you up."

"That's my ax, man," Clayton said. "Had

to get it."

"Dumb," Beat Box said. "Dead dumb."

They walked until the tunnel wall opened to a narrow archway. They stepped inside, Beat Box first. He pointed to a ladder of iron bars that ran up a narrow concrete hole. Clayton looked up. On the other end was a half-moon of light with faces crowding the opening.

"Come on," Beat Box said.

"I can't climb," Clayton said.

Beat Box shrugged. "All right. Hope you like rats."

Clayton watched Beat Box's hands grab the bars as his legs climbed. Beat Box had a steady climbing rhythm and was moving away from him.

He was already grabbing and climbing the grungy, rusty metal rungs. He was grabbing and telling himself, *It's not so high. It's not so high.*

He imagined his body moving like the lizard. His shoulders shifting left and right, left and right, while his hind legs pushed his body upward. He grunted and pulled himself up in what he told himself was "lizard rhythm." The lid to the manhole was now completely removed, making the half-moon above him a round disk of blue afternoon sky.

Beat Box climbed out of the hole.

When Clayton's hands ran out of rungs, he was at the top. Hands reached down and pulled him out of the hole. He covered his eyes for a few seconds. The light from outside was too bright after having been in the tunnel.

He lay on concrete. It took a while before he could sit up.

His breath hadn't caught up and he panted from the climbing. Still, Clayton was glad to see the outside. Glad to be sitting on sidewalk concrete and not on the ledge in the tunnel. Even with his pants ripped at the knee, and his hands scratched up, smelling like sour metal.

Train Ear pushed the manhole cover over the hole and started to walk away. Cool Papa's porkpie hat sat on his head. At least Train Ear had held on to Cool Papa's hat.

Still, he hated Train Ear.

WHAT HE TOLD HIMSELF

The Beats laughed and jumped around like the wolf pack Clayton imagined when he'd first seen them so many train stations ago. His lungs still sore, Clayton got up off the sidewalk and trotted after them. He didn't laugh with them, but to anyone looking on, he was in their pack.

The boys crisscrossed between streets and avenues until they found another train station with trains running in all directions.

Train Ear and Jelly Bones hopped over turnstiles like gymnasts vaulting a pommel horse. Beat Box and Boom Box ducked under the turnstile bars. Clayton took his MetroCard from his pants pocket, swiped it, and then walked through. He had two more fares left on his card.

He followed his grandfather's hat and the Beat Boys down the steps to the main platform.

"Which way?" Jelly Bones asked Train Ear. "Midtown, where suits have money?"

"And cops," Train Ear said. "Blue on every corner."

"Uptown, then," Boom Box said.

Clayton said, "We could go to Washington Square Park. They play the blues down there."

"We don't play the blues," Train Ear said. "What's that? Old-time music?"

"Blues is all right," Clayton said. "Everybody's got the blues."

"Sounds like crying-time music," Jelly Bones said. "We're not crybabies. We're Beat Boys."

Train Ear said to Beat Box, "Make some noise!"

Beat Box made crying sounds to a record-scratching beat.

Clayton said, "All right," like their teasing was nothing. Still, he knew he was a bluesman and that he had to get back to his plan. He said, "Look. I gotta go. I gotta find the Bluesmen."

"The Bluesmen?" Train Ear said. "Forget the Bluesmen. Stay with us."

"We could mix some tunes," Beat Box

said. "Me on beatbox. You on harmonica."

"Blues harp."

"Angels play harps, man." Jelly Bones said "man" the way Clayton said it, which was how Cool Papa said it. But Jelly Bones didn't know that. Only Clayton knew. Like he knew it was time to follow his plan and find the Bluesmen.

"You see how we're making money," Train Ear said. "Why you want to mess that up? Forget the blues."

No. Clayton didn't say it out loud, but "No" popped into his head. He might not have a gutbucket cry or a round-the-corner-and-back-again bend, but he couldn't let go of the blues any more than he could let go of Cool Papa.

"All right," Train Ear said. "Go. We got dollars. We can buy batteries —"

"And a slice!" Boom Box cut in. "One to a man. Extra cheese."

"We don't need Clay Bird and his harp," Train Ear said.

"Fly, Clay Bird," Jelly Bones said.

Then they all went, "Caw! Caw! Caw!" But as soon as Clayton caught Beat Box's eye, Beat Box stopped cawing.

"You should be down with us," Beat Box said.

"My hat," Clayton said to Train Ear. He

held out his hand.

"*My* hat," Train Ear said back.

"Quit playing, man," Clayton said. "Give me my hat back. I gotta get downtown."

Train Ear smiled his mean, hard smile. "If you can take it from me, you can have it."

Clayton didn't have a running start like he did when he snatched the hat from the girl in his backyard who stole Cool Papa's treasures. Instead, he jumped up and reached. But Train Ear stepped back swiftly and Clayton came away with nothing.

"Give me my hat."

"Yeah, man," Beat Box said. "Give him the old hat."

Train Ear cocked his head sharp. That was his "no."

Beat Box said, "Clay Bird was down with us. We made more tips with him. At least give him the hat."

"If he was with us, he'd be with us. Instead of looking for the blues."

"Yeah, Clay Bird. Play with us," Jelly Bones said.

"Play us some pizza money."

Beat Box didn't say anything. Boom Box slugged his twin. Beat Box slugged him back. Train Ear glared at Beat Box. Beat Box looked down.

Clayton Byrd said, "Gimme the hat. Let me go."

Train Ear smiled.

Clayton knew better than to beg for his hat. He'd seen how it went at school when one kid took another kid's stuff. *Look sharp. Be cool.* Cool like when he had wanted that solo with the Bluesmen but felt it slipping away from him. It wasn't easy, wanting something badly and playing it off like it didn't matter. But that was all he could do. He was no match against the wiry, taller, hard-faced teen.

Train Ear removed Cool Papa Byrd's hat from his head. He eyed it, ran his finger around the brim, then looked at Clayton. He stepped to the edge of the platform, held his arm out to the track. Twirling the hat on one finger.

Clayton's heart leapt and sank. But his feet remained still.

His hat.

Cool Papa Byrd's hat. The last piece of Cool Papa Byrd.

If he tried to snatch the hat, Train Ear would throw it out onto the express track. Out into the filthy, rusty, rat-ridden tracks with live rails made to "fry him up" if he tried to go after it. If a train came along, the train wind would sail the hat off Train

Ear's finger. Either way, Cool Papa's porkpie hat would fly out to the train tracks, where Clayton would have no hope of getting it back.

Train Ear gave him a mean, squirrely smile.

Cool, sharp, angry, defeated, Clayton turned on his heel. He walked away with his harp in his pocket, and his empty school bag on his back. He walked away from Beat Box, whom he liked. Away from Boom Box and Jelly Bones, who were okay. And away from Train Ear, who he hated.

Let them go uptown. Let them take that old hat and throw it where the train'll crush it and crush it good. He didn't care — although he did. This was just what he told himself so he could keep walking in the direction of the downtown train.

IN THE MIDST OF THE SWARM

Clayton landed where he needed to be to carry out his plan. The downtown platform. He felt a draft of hot air from the tunnel, a gust left in the wake of the train he'd just missed. That explained why he was nearly the only person standing on the platform. The other, a homeless man, lay across the bench laughing and talking to himself.

Clayton moved away.

Being alone didn't bother him. It was being *seen* as a lone kid that bothered him. He didn't worry for long.

A swarm of yellow and brown surrounded him, like the swarm of bees that had surrounded Pablo de Pablo in the bedtime book. Except these weren't killer bees, but a swarm of school kids of all sizes and grades in brown and gold uniforms. The platform seemed to narrow. He got jostled and squished by pushing, darting kids with full book bags and unleashed energy. They were everywhere. Older kids in groups. Younger kids with their watchers. All on their way home.

Clayton was in the midst of the swarm, although he wasn't a part of them. *Better to blend in than to stand out alone,* he told himself.

To his left he spied a cello case. Then violin cases slung on backs. And it occurred to him: They took band! Their school had band! Unlike his school, where they only had a songbook full of stupid happy songs.

It took a few seconds, but he finally noticed that "they," the kids with the instruments, were girls. He moved closer to where they stood. He didn't know why and he certainly didn't plan to talk to them. And yet another thing occurred to him. He'd never been around kids who actually played instruments — except for Beat Box, even though technically, Beat Box didn't play a musical instrument. Beat Box *was* his own musical instrument.

Clayton went a little closer and said, "Hey."

He didn't mean to do that! It was too late to look away.

The girl with the cello case looked over at him, waited, and said, "Hey."

The other girls laughed.

Clayton pointed to the hard case on wheels with a head and a body, which looked like a little brother leaning into his taller sister. He liked the way she held on to the case, but didn't struggle with it. Like the case, the instrument was a part of her. "You play that?" he asked.

"No," one of the violinists said. "She takes it for rides on the subway."

"Funny," Clayton said.

The violinists laughed.

The cellist nodded to Clayton's question.

"Cool," Clayton said. "Cool."

He felt a breeze blowing from behind. "Train," he said to himself. Or so he thought.

"What?" the cellist asked.

He cleared his throat. "The train's coming," he said.

The cellist waited. Like she wanted him to say something more.

He wanted to ask her about her ax. If she plucked the strings or used a bow. Could she play by ear, like he did, or did she only read notes? But he didn't feel like being laughed at by her friends.

"All right," he said. "Later, ma—" He stopped himself. "Bye."

Clayton pushed through some brown and gold sweaters to get away from the cellist and her friends. He hadn't planned on talking to any girl.

He had to meet up with the Bluesmen. Go on the road. Work on bending his notes. He had a plan.

Finally, the train pulled into the station. Clayton felt his pocket for his blues harp, and then pushed his way onto the downtown train.

In Search of the Bluesmen

When the downtown train reached West Fourth Street station, Clayton was the first to push his way through the doors. He ran up the first set of steps, and the next and the next until he was at the exit and onto the street. Only then did he stop long enough to breathe.

Sixth Avenue in the Village! The heart of the Village. Every fifth person had a guitar slung over his back. The Blue Note was on one side of West Third Street and the Village Underground was on the other side.

It was Friday, the day the Bluesmen would be in the park. This was his last chance to catch them. Maybe Cool Papa's spirit would join them. Maybe he was now the blues in the air. That thought made Clayton hopeful.

Clayton knew the way to the park. He walked briskly up West Third Street, trying to ignore the hunger that had caught up to him. Hunger and soreness from running, climbing, wailing on his blues harp, and plain old not-eating.

He reached into his bag for the pack of peanut butter crackers that Train Ear had crushed. He pried open the package carefully, afraid to drop a crumb. He was so hungry. He tilted his head back and shook out the smashed bits of peanut butter and orange crackers in his mouth until he emptied the pack.

The crumbly, gummy bits of nothing only made him hungrier.

He shook his bag for change but there were no coins. No bills. Train Ear had taken every penny. And Cool Papa's hat.

Clayton was now angry. Angry and hungry. It didn't help that the smells of pizza, sausages, and hot dogs taunted him at every corner. His belly was scraping empty, so empty he could howl.

Instead he said, "I want a slice of pizza, but I'll take a candy bar." He repeated those words as he walked up West Third Street. Repeated them until they became his blues riff and he could hear Wah-Wah Nita's hot electric licks whine in between his lyrics.

A voice reached out, as if to grab him. "Say, kid." The voice had a long arm, its hand shaking a paper cup. "Kid. Say, kid."

Clayton didn't stop. He didn't look to see the face that came with the voice. Cool Papa said, *Look sharp. Be cool,* but Clayton put some jet in his step. Sharp and fast was better.

He was nearing the park and walked straight and purposefully while college students going to and from classes ambled or hurried around him. The Bluesmen and the road were calling him like the sea had called Pablo de Pablo. Except, unlike the boy in the bedtime book, Clayton would not return.

The archway was white and magnificent, even from the opposite side of the park. Big Washington Square Park. It didn't seem so big before, when he was a part of the band. But alone, the park was big. While it wasn't dark, it would soon be dark. He had to find the Bluesmen before the sun went down and people wondered why a boy was walking around in the Village in the dark.

He entered the park. The last time he was there, Cool Papa was at his side, taking big strides like he owned the grand white arch that they'd pass through. A blues king, not a sickly old man, barely making it.

The last time he was in the park with Cool Papa, he'd played *When, Cool Papa, when?* on his harp. Now all he could think was, *Why, Cool Papa, why?*

Clayton walked past the dog run, the chess players, and the skateboarders along the walkway. He made his way to the fountain, the spot where Cool Papa usually played with the Bluesmen.

The lanterns hadn't turned on yet.

Clayton didn't see a crowd of blues lovers gathered at the fountain, or the Bluesmen. Instead, a piano sat in the spot where Cool Papa and the Bluesmen once played. A man whose face was covered by long hair, and a full and long beard, hunched over the keyboard, pounding away. The piano sounded watery, like it had been left out in the rain more than once. No matter what the man played, a drowning sound warbled out from the piano's strings and hammers.

Clayton waited for the piano player to finish. It was an old song that Clayton couldn't name. But it was a long song. And the piano man had a few listeners, but not the crowd that came out to hear Cool Papa and the Bluesmen.

Finally, the bearded piano dude finished

his melody with wobbly, dying chords. No trills. Only a handful of college students and dog walkers stepped up to his tip box and dropped in a few bills. Clayton felt a little bad about not having any love to drop in the box, but Train Ear had taken all of his money. He stepped up to the piano dude.

"Hey, man. That was cool," Clayton said, although it sounded weird to him. "Did the Bluesmen play yet?"

He was hopeful that he'd get in on their first set.

"The Bluesmen?" the man asked. Up close, his skin was tough and scaly.

"The guys that play the blues with Cool Papa. The guys who're usually here. Jack Rabbit Jones on keyboard. Big Mike on bass. Hector Santos on whatever he can hit. The Bluesmen."

The man looked up to the sky. "Those cats."

Clayton was glad the man knew the Bluesmen. "Yeah, man. Those cats," Clayton said.

"You missed them. I heard they won't be back till spring, after the rains. When the sun's here to stay for a while. Figure on late May."

"Gone?" Clayton asked. He started to count backward in his head. *Had it been two weeks?* "You're sure?"

"How d'you think I got this spot? Been waiting for a while."

Clayton just stood there. Stood there while the piano man began another wobbly tune. He stood there. Not thinking. Not breathing. Just aching. Aching in his gut where he'd been mule-kicked by everything gone wrong.

The piano melody sounded bad. Really bad.

Clayton took in a breath from deep down. Deep down where a good blues bend would start from. He drew in his air, blew it out, and let it go.

The plan was no plan.

The Bluesmen were gone.

Cool Papa's spirit wasn't in the air. Cool Papa was gone. Gone for good.

There was nowhere to go but home.

GOING DOWN

Clayton walked the short walk to the West Fourth Street station and trotted down to the turnstiles. He swiped the last fare on his card and pushed himself through. He sang to himself as he went down the station steps, the steps to the platform, to the middle mezzanine, and to the uptown express, where he couldn't get any lower. He'd heard the words a hundred times. Played the song even more. But those were just the notes he heard and played. What he felt was that he'd hit bottom.

It was a double-shift night. His mother wouldn't be home by the time he made it

147

back to his neighborhood. But he wasn't in the clear. She'd probably already called Omar's mother. She probably knew by now that he hadn't gone to Omar's house like he was supposed to. He also hadn't thought about the school letter proclaiming his absence that would reach his mailbox the next morning. Those letters arrived awfully fast! Nor had he thought about the angel saltshaker smashed to pieces on the floor where he'd left it. Maybe he could slip into the house. Clean it up. Say it was an accident. Then go to Omar's house and wait for his mother, as if the plan and the day never happened.

But he slid his hand into his pocket and felt his blues harp. His silver blues harp. Once he'd snatched it from the dresser drawer of silky underthings, he could never put it back. Once he'd smashed his mother's saltshaker angel into a million pieces, there was no putting it back together, or lying about what happened.

Every direction his brain pinged led to dead ends. He'd have to face his mother. Tell her everything. Or almost everything.

A warm wisp of tunnel air blew in his face and then passed by him. He saw a glow growing against the white wall tiles. The train was pulling into the station.

People pushed their way out of the open doors, and Clayton stepped inside the train. A car full of work people with tired, flat faces took up nearly all of the seats and standing space. No one wanted the empty seat next to the huge mound of a homeless man in dirty clothes. The snoring man's mouth gaped sloppily like some huge beast's. Dirty clothes and newspapers covered his body. His feet were wrapped in plastic bags.

At least, Clayton thought, the homeless man didn't smell bad. At all. He didn't want to stand, so he sat in the empty seat, and sat as far away as he could. He couldn't smell anything, but put his hands over his nose, just in case.

The train chugged along from station to station. Still no empty seat to change to.

He felt uneasy next to the homeless man, and hoped really hard as the train pulled into the next stop. He waited to see if anyone would get off and if he could run to take the seat. As Clayton's luck went, more people boarded the train than departed. Just as the conductor said, "Stand clear of the closing doors, please —"

"BEATS ON! BEATS ON!"

He saw them push their way inside the train car. The standing people shrank away from the pushing boys, giving them a space to work.

"EVERY RIDER, CLAP YOUR HANDS! EVERY RIDER, CLAP YOUR HANDS!"

Hat.

Clayton Byrd was already out of his seat, striding toward the hat.

"Well, look who's back!" Jelly Bones said.

"Yo! Clay Bird!" Beat Box shouted.

"Clay Bird!" Boom Box said. "Get down with us."

Clayton told Train Ear, "I want my hat."

"Give him the hat," Beat Box said. "It's his, man."

"Yeah, man," Boom Box said. "Give it to him."

Jelly Bones said, "Give him the hat, man. Let's make some coins."

Train Ear took the hat off his head. He said, "All right," in all vowels, no consonants. "It's yours, my man. After you play. Word." He put Cool Papa's hat back on his head.

The Beat Boys believed Train Ear. They did their shuffle and clap to make a space for Clayton to join them. Clayton didn't believe Train Ear. Still, he shuffled. Right foot. Left foot. No hop. He took his blues harp out of his pocket. Wiped it, slicked it up in his mouth, and joined them in between the beat. He blew deep, hard, but never took his eyes off Train Ear. He didn't care how he'd do it, but he wasn't getting off the train without his hat.

A pair of cops got on at the next stop.

"BEATS OUT!" Train Ear shouted.

The boys turned and ran to the other end of the train, bumping into riders everywhere.

"Sorry," Clayton said. "Sorry." But he had his eye on his grandfather's hat, and pushed and ran to keep up with it.

The homeless man stood up like a grizzly on hind legs. His newspapers fell away. A gold police shield hung around his neck.

The Beat Boys and Clayton Byrd were pinned at both ends.

WITHOUT A WARNING

They gave their names to Writing Cop. Beat Box and Boom Box's real names rhymed. Jelly Bones's real name didn't fit him. Clayton didn't hear Train Ear's real name. He didn't care.

Train Ear didn't look so big standing next to the cop. "Aw, man," he pleaded, his hard mouth all teeth.

Clayton hadn't seen Train Ear smile like that. An all-out grin, trying to make his face look innocent.

"Let us off with a warning."

The cop kept writing in his thick pad.

Jelly Bones said, "We were just dancing. Making the people happy."

"More like kicking the people in the face," Young Square Cop said; he was short and square, built like one of those guys who blocked tackles in college football. "We call it reckless endangerment, soliciting, and disturbing the peace."

"Aw, come on, officer. Please." He smiled real hard.

Writing Cop shook his head. "No more warnings for you guys. How many warnings before you get it?" He poked Train Ear in the chest with his pen.

The poke was hard. Train Ear shrank when his skinny chest caved in.

Writing Cop told him, "These are kids. You're" — he glanced at his writing pad — "an adult by law."

Clayton spoke up. "Then can I go? This is my first warning."

The Beat Boys laughed at Clayton's innocence. Train Ear swore.

"Shut it," Grizzly Bear said. He moved closer to Writing Cop. He pointed to Clayton. "This one might be coming from school. He didn't get on with them."

Clayton didn't say yes or no, although he was glad he had sat next to the cop when he got on the train. He kept his mouth shut, but he looked hopeful. He just wanted to get back on the train, beat his mother home, eat, and wash up, in that order. His stomach ached from hunger.

The others caught his hopeful look, and Boom Box said, "That's cold, Clay Bird. You know you're down with us."

"Told you," Train Ear said. "Told you, but no one listens."

Beat Box looked at Clayton, and then he looked down.

Writing Cop said, "I see a book bag, but I don't see any books." He shook his head no to Grizzly Bear. "He gets a pickup along with his compadres."

Clayton did as he was told and raised his hands above his head. The last time he'd done that was in gym for jumping jacks. Grizzly Bear patted Clayton down. Arms, underarms, torso, backside, down his legs from top to bottom, inside and outside. Then the jacket pocket. Clayton's hand went for his pocket, but Grizzly Bear said, "You don't want to do that, kid."

Clayton was already breathing hard and fast. The prospect of having his blues harp taken was more than he could bear. His legs weakened, but somehow he remained on his two feet. He looked up at the big cop. His eyes said, *Please.*

The cop took out the silver blues harp,

looked at it, looked at Clayton, then dropped it into a larger plastic bag. He took the book bag next, opened it, shook it, pulled it inside out, and dropped it inside the bag as well.

"Sorry, kid."

"Look at the baby bird. Baby bird's gonna cry," Jelly Bones said, laughing.

"You," Grizzly Bear said to Jelly Bones. He didn't have to finish his thought.

Jelly Bones shut his mouth fast and tight in mid-laugh.

Clayton couldn't help it. His eyes filled up. One tear fell. Then another.

Beat Box had nothing to drop inside a plastic bag, but Boom Box's dead boom box went into one. Jelly Bones's fuzzy white Kangol cap went reluctantly into another. The truth was, the cap had stopped being white long before Clayton had first spotted it and the wolf pack on the platform hours ago. It was only now that Clayton could see the cap's color. Dingy, but not as dirty as Train Ear's tank top.

Clayton wiped his eyes and then shifted them to Grizzly Bear without turning his head. He watched Grizzly Bear take Cool Papa's hat off Train Ear's head and drop it in the plastic bag along with the mess of dollar bills and coins he removed from Train

Ear's pockets.

"Yo! That's my money!" Train Ear said.

"Our money!" the others said.

Clayton wiped his face fast. "That's my hat!"

Writing Cop said to Clayton, "So, you *do* know these guys."

Clayton almost said, "I don't." Which was true. He didn't know them like he knew Omar. Or the lizard that darted in and out of the rock den inside the cage next to his desk.

Clayton said nothing.

"Okay, Twinkle Toes," Writing Cop said to Train Ear, Jelly Bones, Boom Box, Beat Box, and Clayton, "Looks like you ballerinas have all earned an official escort to the ball. But first, the bracelets."

One by one, Clayton and the Beat Boys filed out of the police van and were led into the station, their hands behind their backs, bound by plastic strip handcuffs.

Cool Papa's words had been with Clayton from the time he'd sat on the train. *Look sharp. Be cool.* But those words wouldn't help him. The plastic strips choked off the blood flowing to his hands. With his head hung low and his chin on his chest, Clayton walked the line carrying within him all he felt Cool Papa had left to give him: ghost notes, wails, and the moans from deep down that Cool Papa made in between his once-hot guitar licks.

Clayton felt only the numbness in his wrists and the wail in his gut. He could cry. Deep down he could really cry.

When they came upon a small room, Young Square Cop cut the handcuffs off Clayton, Beat Box, Boom Box, and Jelly Bones, but he didn't cut Train Ear's handcuffs.

Clayton rubbed his wrists and wiped his eyes. Beat Box kicked Clayton's sneaker. "Quit it, yo."

Clayton didn't know if he meant quit crying or quit rubbing his wrists. He didn't care.

Clayton entered the small room first. Its cinder-block walls had been painted and repainted in a bright whitish-yellow that made Clayton's eyes hurt. He sat on one of the two benches.

Writing Cop said, "You better pray your guardian angel shows up before nine. Family court is closed for the weekend and the social worker will be gone. If your guardian doesn't show, you stay until Monday."

"In this room?" Clayton asked.

The boys all laughed.

The cop said, "Not here. You'll be on the bus to detention. Your guardian can pick you up there. Except you," he said to Train Ear, whose hands were still bound behind his back.

"What did I do?" Train Ear asked, although the time to act innocent was over. "Why I got these on?"

Writing Cop said, "You're going someplace special."

"Aw, man," Train Ear said.

"Let's go," Grizzly Bear said.

Grizzly, Writing Cop, Young Square Cop, and Train Ear left.

Clayton stopped wiping his face but he couldn't stop rubbing his wrists. He could still see the impression of the plastic strips that dug into his skin. He still felt the strain in his shoulders from having his arms and hands behind his back.

The bench was hard but the waiting was harder. He wanted his mother to come soon, but he didn't want to face her.

If ever he needed the deep-down blues, now was his time.

His hand went for his pocket, but his blues harp wasn't there. He closed his eyes to hear the blues. To hear the words about searching for "up" when everything around him pulled him down. It was his own blues. His own words. His own voice.

"Yo, Clay Bird. You still crying?" Beat Box asked.

Clayton knew the boy's name. His real name. But he was still Beat Box to Clayton.

"You scared to go to detention?" Boom Box asked.

"You're not?" Clayton asked back.

Beat Box shrugged. "We're inside. Better than the cold. They're going to feed us something." He shrugged again.

"He scared of that whipping from his mama or his pops. You got a pops, Clay Bird?" Boom Box asked.

"He doesn't live with us," Clayton said.

"Ours don't either," Beat Box said.

"Or our moms," Boom Box said.

Jelly Bones closed his eyes. "Wake me when they take us to D."

Beat Box said, "Wish you had your harp, man. Wish we could make some noise."

Then outside the door Clayton heard, "Ms. Juanita Byrd? Yes. We have your son. He's here."

GUARDIAN ANGEL

When the officer called, "Clayton Byrd," Clayton stood up. He turned mostly to Beat Box but fumbled for something to say.

Beat Box spoke up first. "Looks like your guardian angel flew in."

Guardian angel, Clayton thought.

"You out, man?" Boom Box asked.

"Yeah, man," Clayton said. "I'm out."

Boom Box offered a nod and said, "Peace, Clay Bird."

"Peace," Clayton said.

Jelly Bones snored.

"Play that harp, man," Beat Box said.

"Make some noise," Clayton said back, although he thought Beat Box, Boom Box, and Jelly Bones could use some blues.

Clayton stepped into the hallway. He could hear Beat Box and Boom Box going "caw, caw, caw" behind him. He wanted to smile, but his mother stood before him in her white hospital shoes.

"Clayton," she whispered. Her voice was crumbly and soft.

"Hi, Mom," he said.

Her face was red. Puffy. He stepped toward her.

"Are you all right?" she asked.

He nodded, then said, "I'm okay."

She exhaled and looked up to the ceiling, patting her foot, wringing her hands. She wiped her face, wiped her eyes, and exhaled again.

"Clayton . . ."

He waited for more. Waited for what he had coming. She looked so different to him.

"Where have you been? What are you doing in the city? What's all this about running with a street gang? Why are your pants ripped? Why didn't you go to Omar's? What were you thinking? Jail! Of all places, jail?"

Words poured out of her like air gushing from a balloon. Her voice was now anchored, clear and fast. Clayton heard only the sounds of her words coming at him.

"And you're filthy. You think you're in

161

trouble? You don't know trouble. Wait until I get you home."

"Ms. Byrd." The desk sergeant spoke up. "Property's right down the hall." He pointed and they followed. Clayton's mother was still talking.

"Name," the property officer stated.

Clayton spoke up. "Clayton Byrd."

The officer got up, went to a cubby, and returned with a plastic bag containing the book bag and the blues harp, which he placed on the desk.

Ms. Byrd glared at the bag and its contents. At least some of the anger that Clayton had felt came back to him.

"Sign," the officer said to Ms. Byrd.

Clayton took the bag.

"There's a hat back there too," Clayton said. "It's mine."

"Sorry," the clerk said. "I can only give you what's in your bag."

"But the brown hat's mine. I don't want the money. I just want the hat. It's mine. That dude just took it."

"What hat?" Ms. Byrd asked. "You mean that old brown hat? Your grandfather's hat? As far as I'm concerned, officer, you can keep it. And you!" she said to Clayton. "You just wait."

She was back, Clayton thought. The

mother who took his things was back, and the mother who might have been a little sorry had disappeared.

The property clerk went back to a cubby, opened the plastic bag containing the hat and the money, and pulled out the hat.

"Take your hat," he said.

"But officer, I said I don't want him to have it," Clayton's mother said.

"It's his hat," the officer said. "You just confirmed it. What you do when you leave is up to you."

Clayton gave the officer a nod and followed his mother out of the police station. He wiped the inside of the felt hat. Wiped it good and then waved it in the night air as he walked to keep up with his mother.

"Put your seat belt on," she said when he got in the car. Clayton watched the clock on the dashboard from the time they got into the car until they arrived home. That was all she said for thirty-seven minutes. Which was fine with Clayton.

When they pulled into their driveway, Ms. Byrd said, "First, I get a call from Omar's mom, and we are both hysterical, trying to figure out what happened to you. When I get home, the school had left a message on the answering machine saying you were absent. Then, I get a call from the police.

Clayton, you have no idea what you put us all through. Omar. His mother. Your father. Your aunts and uncles. Me."

Clayton took it in. He tried to imagine Omar waiting for him on the afternoon school bus. Omar's mom asking, "Where's Clayton?" His mother speeding home to find him. His family worried. None of this had been part of his plan.

His mother was still talking. "You have no idea. You have no idea what you've done to yourself —" Each word in its own box. "You have no idea what you've done to your life. All because of that thing." She meant his harp. "And that hat. I ought to throw it where it belongs. In the trash."

Her words made whatever remorse he felt disappear. "You can't take my hat!" Clayton shouted. "It's all I have left."

"You broke my angel!" she shouted at him.

"You took my blues harp!"

"My mother gave me those angels. My mother!" she screamed at him. Not like his mother, but like a little girl.

"Well you took EVERYTHING from me. You didn't care where Cool Papa's things went. You just gave them away like they were nothing."

"He was my father, and those things were mine to get rid of."

"He was my grandfather, and he left those things for me," Clayton said. He had never said so much to his mother. Now, he couldn't stop. "You hated your own father. You didn't love him."

She pointed her finger at him. "Boy, you don't know what you're talking about."

"You gave away his guitars, and those were mine. You gave away his favorite guitar, and he named it after you."

"Do you think it's easy, growing up without a father? Do you think it's easy having a father who loves his guitars and the road more than he loves you?"

"At least I loved Cool Papa the way he was."

"So now you think you know something. Out in the world. End up in jail. I'm trying to save you from what's out there. I'm trying to save you from yourself."

Her face was getting puffy again, but Clayton didn't care. He said, "I don't want you to save me. I want Cool Papa!"

She pointed her finger at him again and started to say something. Then she turned her head away to look out the window. "Boy. Go inside. Run your bath."

Ms. Byrd and Mr. Miller

Clayton was now clean, dry, and wearing pajamas. He didn't want to go downstairs but he was hungry. He crept almost halfway down the stairs when he heard his mother say, "I can't deal with him right now. Come and get your son."

Clayton didn't wait for her to tell him to get dressed or to pack. He was in his room throwing clothes and comic books into his overnight bag. The usual things he packed when he stayed overnight at his father's house. He didn't bother to change out of his pajamas. He kept them on and yanked a baseball jacket off its hanger. He'd never worn it before. Baseball was his father's thing, not his. But the jacket was new and

166

clean and he was ready for new and clean. Still, he put Cool Papa's porkpie hat in the overnight bag. Cool Papa's hat would get crushed in the small bag, but it had survived so much.

Clayton put on his baseball jacket, tucked his blues harp in the jacket's deep pocket, and then sat by the window.

Within minutes his father's car was parking in the driveway behind his mother's car. He watched his father get out and walk toward the front door. He pulled back the curtain and waved.

His father looked up to Clayton's room, stood for a few seconds under the porch light, and waved back.

Clayton grabbed his overnight bag and ran down the stairs.

His mother stood before the door, her arms folded.

"Now, you just wait a minute," she told Clayton. Then she opened the door and let his father in. Mr. Miller kissed her on the cheek and stepped inside.

"Jailbird," his father said to Clayton.

"Dad," Clayton said, feeling foolish.

"That's not funny, Albert," his mother said.

"I'm sorry," Clayton's father told her, although he didn't look too sorry. To Clayton he said, "Kiss your mother, and get in the car."

Clayton gave his father a look. "Aw, man."

"Kiss your mother," his father repeated. "I'll be a minute."

Clayton sighed. "A minute" meant five or ten.

Clayton turned to his mother. She looked at him. He looked at her. She tilted her face to the side and he kissed her quickly where his father had kissed her.

"Bye," he said, and turned to walk away.

"You just wait," his mother said, and wrapped her arms around him.

After more than he could stand, Clayton said, "Okay, Mom." He eased his way out of her arms, gave his father a slug, and walked toward the car.

Ms. Byrd and Mr. Miller watched Clayton open the car door and get inside. They turned to each other.

"Who are you really angry at?" Mr. Miller asked. "Clayton, me, or Papa?"

"Don't call him that. He was nobody's Papa. Least of all yours."

"I beg to differ," Mr. Miller said. "He was Clayton's 'Cool Papa.' He loved that boy and that boy loves him. And he was pretty good to me."

"Well, he was no father to me."

Mr. Miller shrugged and raised his eyebrows the way Clayton shrugged and raised his eyebrows. "Maybe. But you can't erase Papa and who he was. You got to let that boy love Papa. Or you get this."

"You're making excuses for his behavior," Ms. Byrd said. "Acting up in school, then ditching school and joining up with some gang and" — she took a breath, shook her head, blinked her eyes like someone imagining an awful, awful sight — "getting arrested by the police. By the police." Her voice quaked like it had in the police station.

Mr. Miller grabbed her hands. "I know. I know. We are very lucky."

"And he broke my mother's angel!" Ms. Byrd snatched her hands away. Her voice was once again in control of itself.

"What?"

"He didn't just break it," Ms. Byrd went on. "No. Your son smashed it to pieces so it can't be fixed."

Mr. Miller looked at her. Hard. "Juanita Byrd, do you hear yourself? *Do you?*"

"He's out of control," Ms. Byrd said.

"He's hurting," Mr. Miller said.

"That boy doesn't know the meaning of hurting."

Mr. Miller smiled. "Tough talk, Wah-Wah

Nita. Your face is still puffy from crying."

Ms. Byrd pointed her finger at Mr. Miller. "Do not call me that."

"Why? Reminds you of Papa?"

"He wasn't your Papa."

"But he was Clayton's Papa," Mr. Miller said. "Look, Juanita. We can do this till the cows come home. But we need to talk. All of us. We have to face it. We're all hurting. We're all angry. Now, go back inside. Finish crying. I'll bring him back when he's ready." Then he added, "When you're ready too."

BELIEVE

"Son," his father said when he got in the car. "Clayton."

"I'm hungry," Clayton said. He was cold, too. And tired.

"Don't worry. I got you," his father said. "Fish sticks and spaghetti." He turned to Clayton. "All right with you?"

"All right," Clayton said. His father didn't make his favorite meal the way Cool Papa did. Cool Papa fried the fish sticks and poured ketchup on the spaghetti. His father nuked the fish sticks and used marinara. But that was all right. Spaghetti and fish sticks was what he wanted.

"We have to talk," his father said. "We have to talk."

Clayton was tired and hungry. "Can we talk tomorrow?"

His father shook his head no and said, "You can't do that, Clayton. You can't take off like that." His father spoke calmly. Clearly. His voice didn't break like his mother's, but Clayton could feel the difference from how his father usually spoke. "You're old enough to know what could happen to you out there. Suppose instead of, 'Ms. Byrd, your son has been picked up,' your mother heard, 'Ms. Byrd, there's been an accident.' Suppose instead of coming to get you, suppose I was coming to see you at the morgue." His father looked straight ahead. He was still shaking his head.

Clayton didn't know what to say to any of that. None of it had occurred to him. Only getting through the day. He let his father drive. Then he asked, "Why does she hate Cool Papa?"

Albert Miller cleared his throat, wiped his eyes, and said, "Your mother doesn't hate her father."

Clayton looked at his father. The truth was one thing he could count on from Mr. Miller. *Why won't you marry my mother?* *Because she won't marry me.* Now, his

172

father was lying to him.

"She hates everything about him," he said.

"Not everything."

"That's bull."

"Watch it, jailbird."

Clayton sighed.

"He hurt the little girl in her. Too many times. You know about being hurt too many times."

Clayton knew.

His father said, "The hurt just never went away. It's like she's still that little girl waiting at the window."

Clayton felt his father's eyes on him, as if he expected him to say something. Clayton said nothing. He didn't care about his mother's hurt.

"You're mad at her like she's been mad at Papa."

Clayton still said nothing.

They were getting close to his father's house.

"I heard about the yard sale," his father said. "And while I know you're still mad at her, I want you to think about one thing."

"What." He didn't really ask because he didn't want to know.

"Your mother gave you two things I never had: a father and a grandfather."

Clayton's father parked and shut down

the engine once they pulled into the garage. He unbuckled his seat belt, although Clayton left his seat belt locked.

"What?" his father asked.

"Can I ask you something?"

His father raised his eyebrows and shrugged. "Anything."

"Cool Papa wasn't sick like Grandmama. Why'd he die like that?"

His father thought for a minute. Clayton wanted to hear what his father would say more than he wanted the actual answer.

"Son," his father said. "I don't know."

Clayton sat, both let down and relieved. Still, he liked the way his father said it. Plain and true. *I don't know.*

"Hey." His father slugged his shoulder. "Thought you were hungry."

"I am," Clayton said. "Just one more thing."

"I got all day. All night."

"Okay," Clayton began. "Where do you go when you die? Not your body. Your . . . you. Your spirit. Does it stay and hang around the house or does it go to the places it liked or remembers? Does it go inside things or other people and become something else? Someone else? Dad, where does your spirit go? The part that's you?"

Clayton's father laughed. Laughed real

long. Then stopped.

"I'm not laughing at you," he said. "No . . . I am." He laughed some more. "Clayton, when you finally decide to say something . . ." He caught his breath. "Okay," his father said. "People believe different things. It's all in what you believe. But honestly, Clayton, no one really knows."

Clayton let that sink in. Was it that simple? He thought about what he believed and where he believed Cool Papa's spirit went.

His father tapped him on the shoulder. "Come on."

Clayton undid his seat belt. He reached for his blues harp, deep in his new pocket. He was ready to go inside and tell his father almost everything.

Sometimes a Ghost Note

It seemed as if Clayton had been gone long. Gone out into the world on a small boat. Out to the four corners of the world, answering the sea's call.

Just like the tide had pulled Pablo de Pablo out to sea, the tide pulled Clayton back to shore.

Back to school and Ms. Treadwell's class, with a doctor's note that said he didn't have to read *The Four Corners of the World* in class. Back to his desk, where he sang "This Land Is Your Land" while the lizard darted out from his rock den to feast on Egyptian clover.

Back on the school bus with his best friend, Omar, and with the other kids who still called him "Sleepster."

Back to his block where his mother's house wasn't far from his father's house, and his mother and father no longer seemed so far apart.

Back home, where the house smelled of pork chops, peas, and potatoes — his least favorite meal, but there would be one less angel at the table, and that made Clayton smile. Eventually, that made Juanita Byrd laugh. A little.

"Wash up," his mother told him when he walked through the door. "And put your things away."

He dashed by her so fast, he missed her smile.

Clayton climbed the stairs and pushed open his bedroom door. He stood in the doorway, unable to move. Across the armrest of Cool Papa's watcher's chair lay the old guitar that had once cried and twanged hot electric chords and sometimes a ghost note out into the night. He ran his fingers against the smooth wood, and then up the neck, and down the strings. Finally, he picked up and held the guitar, and tried to remember how Cool Papa used to hold her. Clayton held it tightly with one hand, but looser in the other. He couldn't play her like a bluesman yet, or at all, for that matter, but one day he'd make her laugh and cry. His Wah-Wah Nita.

A NOTE FROM THE AUTHOR

Years ago I saw a video of rapper Doug E. Fresh alternately beatboxing and playing the harmonica in his live show. I was used to hearing the harmonica played in blues and in country-and-western music, but this mash-up clicked instantly for me! Of course, the blues and hip-hop! While the blues wasn't necessarily a young person's music when it was first played, its raw beginnings, tone, and themes conveyed the same feelings of invisibility, swagger, and injustice as hip-hop, its descendant. I knew I would write something about this pairing, but I was in the middle of another novel. Like many fascinations, I tucked it away for later.

I had my mother to thank for my introduction to the blues, among many other musical forms. She played albums by Billie Holiday, T-Bone Walker, Ray Charles, and others while parting and braiding my hair for kindergarten. The music wasn't at all happy or for children. The blues was strictly "grown folks' music." The sun wouldn't come out and shine for Billie Holiday, T-Bone Walker lived in a mean old world, and poor Ray Charles couldn't pay his bills and was always "busted." I couldn't understand why my mother loved this music. Yet she'd talk back to the lyrics and to the sassy, brassy horns in her unique voice. What I didn't know at age five was that my mother, like so many blues lovers, found strength, cunning, humor, and vindication in blues lyrics. Much later, as a graduate student, I'd trace the origin of the blues to West African oral traditions, particularly "call-and-response." In twelve-bar blues, the "call" is seen in *A,* the first line, and is then repeated more or less in the second line, also *A.* The eight bars of the *AA* call are then answered in the following four bars, or *B,* the response.

Call: Trouble, don't you find me; Trouble, leave me alone. [A]
Call: I SAID, Trouble, keep your distance, Trouble; you better leave me alone. [A]
Response: Every time I think I kicked you to the curb, Trouble, I turn around and find you hanging on. [B]

The call-and-response pattern poured out of African Americans of the Deep South in the forms of spirituals, field hollers, work songs, and personal testimonies or narratives. From the late nineteenth century through the early twentieth century, typical blues lyrics spoke of hard work, hard times, broken hearts, and broken people, often accompanied on equally broken-down or handmade instruments. The blues was thought to be low-down and was called "the devil's music."

As African Americans left the South for larger cities in the Great Migration, the blues traveled with them and evolved. Musical instruments were store-bought. The sound and subject matter of the blues became sophisticated, reflecting urban living, while each big city developed its own distinct blues sound. Today the blues is recognized as authentic American music that gave birth to or influenced gospel, rhythm and blues, rock and roll, funk, and country music. Whether I understood the blues or not as a child, I was grateful for my early exposure. When blues legend Willie Mae "Big Mama" Thornton performed at my elementary school in Seaside, California, I had an advantage over my schoolmates. I knew who Thornton was and could sing her version of "Hound Dog" while she performed.

As a teen I couldn't help but love popular music, but I also took note of its changing trends. One night while in college, a friend and I left our dorm at Hofstra University, "dressed to impress" to dance the Hustle at a club in Long Island. Clubs were very strict about their dress code and many advertised a "no sneaker, no hip-hop" policy, referring to both clothing and a style of dance. When we pulled into the parking lot, there were two couples dancing outside. The first couple, two men, did incredible lifts and spins; however, it was the other couple that caught my eye. They looked more ready to play basketball than to dance in a club. The girl wore a faded denim vest and cut-off jeans, and both she and her partner wore high-top sneakers. Although the couple danced the Hustle, it was their hard-swinging partnering, accented with equally hard rock-backs and high-hops that distinguished their athletic style from the smooth, sophisticated glide I was used to seeing and dancing. My friend and I stayed outside in the parking lot to watch the dancers, who weren't welcome inside the club. Months later, the same girl had enrolled at Hofstra. I would see her and a crew of guys (B-boys) body spinning and dancing in the campus quad on pieces of cardboard boxes. She wore the same high-top sneakers, but instead of doing her hip-hop Hustle, she was break dancing.

By the late seventies to the mid-eighties, hip-hop had risen from the underground and trickled into the mainstream with its own style of music, dance, language, art, fashion, and activism. Although the Bronx is credited as its birthplace, the culture spread quickly to the college scene, and Long Island was no exception. The dances I attended as a freshman at Hofstra were a far cry from the dances I attended as a senior in the early hip-hop era. Legendary hip-hop producer Hank Shocklee was a student at Hofstra and was also a much sought-after DJ for black fraternity and sorority dances. It wasn't enough for a DJ to spin records on turntables. The DJ's crew put on a show that included scratching and cutting, mixing, beatboxing, light shows, crowd interaction, and rap battles. Through it all, the hip-hop beat reigned supreme. Once kept on the outside, the sneaker-wearing crowd that ushered in hip-hop — branded a passing fad — continued to dictate popular culture into the twenty-first century.

Fast-forward to decades later. In between writing projects I thought about *Clayton Byrd Goes Underground.* I had main characters, a story idea, and my own brief bout with narcolepsy (a disorder that makes one fall asleep at inappropriate times) to draw on. I had an overall sense of connection between basic blues and old-school hip-hop, such as their mature language and subject matter, use of "signifying" — the art of verbal jousting African American style — and their raw-to-refined evolution, among other similarities. What I was looking for lay beneath the surface of what I knew or could research. It wasn't until I sat in on a blues lecture given by Kathi Appelt at Vermont College of Fine Arts that I felt a tingling in my brain that brought me back to Doug E. Fresh beatboxing and playing the blues harp, another name for the harmonica. The same breath that produced hi-hats and tom-toms through beatboxing also produced trills and wails on the blues harp. Beneath the "down deep" breath was the essential blues cry that Kathi spoke of, but also the holler of a new generation. Both beatboxing and playing the blues harp relied upon inventiveness in a language churned up from the gut and out through breath, throat, tongue, teeth, lips, and spit to amplify the musician's voice and emotional road beyond mere words. I confess that at the moment my brain was firing, I had stopped taking lecture notes and began to lock into the noise and pain that would send Clayton Byrd on his way.

ABOUT THE AUTHOR

Rita Williams-Garcia is the author of the Newbery Honor Book *One Crazy Summer,* which was a winner of the Coretta Scott King Award, a National Book Award finalist, the recipient of the Scott O'Dell Award for Historical Fiction, and a *New York Times* bestseller. The sequels, *P.S. Be Eleven* and *Gone Crazy in Alabama,* were both Coretta Scott King Award winners. She is also the author of six distinguished novels for young adults: *Jumped,* a National Book Award finalist; *No Laughter Here, Every Time a Rainbow Dies* (a *Publishers Weekly* Best Children's Book), and *Fast Talk on a Slow Track* (all ALA Best Books for Young Adults); *Blue Tights;* and *Like Sisters on the Homefront,* a Coretta Scott King Honor Book. Rita Williams-Garcia lives in Jamaica, New York, with her husband and has two adult daughters, Stephanie and Michelle, and a son-in-law, Adam. You can visit her online at www.ritawg.com.

The employees of Thorndike Press hope you have enjoyed this Large Print book. All our Thorndike, Wheeler, and Kennebec Large Print titles are designed for easy reading, and all our books are made to last. Other Thorndike Press Large Print books are available at your library, through selected bookstores, or directly from us.

For information about titles, please call:
  (800) 223-1244

or visit our website at:
  gale.com/thorndike

To share your comments, please write:
  Publisher
  Thorndike Press
  10 Water St., Suite 310
  Waterville, ME 04901